LOVE & FOLLY

LOVE & FOLLY

Selected Fables and Tales of LaFontaine
TRANSLATED BY MARIE PONSOT

Edited and with an Introduction by Benjamin Ivry

Illustrations by Soon Chun Cho

WELCOME RAIN PUBLISHERS New York

Direct any inquiries to:
Welcome Rain Publishers LLC
23 West 26th Street
New York, NY 10010.

Originally published in 1966 by the New American Library, Inc.
under the title SELECTED FABLES AND TALES OF LA FONTAINE

Library of Congress Cataloging-in-Publication Data
La Fontaine, Jean de, 1621-1695.
    [Selections. English. 2002]
    Love & Folly : selected fables and tales of La Fontaine /
translated by Marie Ponsot.
        p. cm.
    Includes index.
    ISBN 1-56649-227-0
    1. La Fontaine, Jean de, 1621-1695—Translations into English.
I. Title: Love et Folly.
    II. Ponsot, Marie. III. Title.
    PQ1811 .E2 2002
    841'.4—dc21   2002016831
    ISBN 1-56649-227-0

Printed in the United States of America
First Edition: March 2002

1 3 5 7 9 10 8 6 4 2

CONTENTS

First and Second Parts
BOOK I

BOOK II

BOOK III

BOOK IV

BOOK V

BOOK VI

Third and Fourth Parts
BOOK VII

BOOK VIII

BOOK IX

BOOK X

BOOK XI

Fifth Part
BOOK XII

TALES AND SHORT STORIES
PART I

PART II

PART III

PART IV

OCCASIONAL VERSE

"DIVERSITY IS MY MOTTO"
On La Fontaine and Marie Ponsot

The French poet Jean de La Fontaine (1621–1695) combined charm and humor in strict poetic form to leave behind a legacy that is still in the process of being fully understood. His most famous works, twelve books of Fables, have been used as school texts for generations of young French readers. Despite the animal characters, the poems show scant interest in natural history, instead being commentaries on human behavior, where the advice is always leavened by Gallic wit. In addition to these versified stories from Aesop and other sources, he also published volumes of bawdy—yet always elegant—tales, and wrote epigrams as well. Because most of his poems were based on source material, some contemporary writers, like Boileau, dismissed him as unoriginal. Certain more recent readers, like the poet Paul Eluard, mistook him for a carping moralist. But the majority treasured what the aphorist Chamfort called his "natural wisdom . . . which seems to have been a lucky development from his own instincts."

Voltaire noted in *The Century of Louis XIV* that La Fontaine was the "only great man of his time" who did not enjoy support from the Sun King. Instead, La Fontaine found a patron in Nicolas Fouquet, the King's superintendent of finances and a noted bon vivant. When Fouquet built Vaux-le-Vicomte, a splendid residence outside Paris, the King saw it as a threat to his supremacy, and jailed him for life. La Fontaine did not abandon his friend, writing poems in Fouquet's honor, although these did not change the King's mind. La Fontaine always relied on private patrons for the basic necessities of food and housing. Attempts at various professions, including the church and law, fell through, so that La Fontaine became what his friend the literary gossip Tallement des Réaux called "a belles-lettres boy who also writes verses." When one patron died after twenty years of steady support, another friend saw the elderly La Fontaine hobbling along a street, and offered him housing. "That's where I was going," (*"J'y allais"*) he replied with typical French resourcefulness.

Always dependent on others, La Fontaine was motivated to create works that pleased and entertained. An assiduous craftsman who only gave the impression of being lazy, he polished his poems until they gleamed. The critic Leo Spitzer—who admired La Fontaine's "concentration, refinement, and refusal of pathos"—pointed to his "transitions," or trains of thought that wind along a seemingly fortuitous path. The real subject of a given poem may only appear gradually, in what might be thought a casual way. This meandering, which winds up in a witty and sensible conclusion, is a particular challenge to reproduce in translation. Then there is the "fluid suavitas," or surface polish and music of the verse itself, which Spitzer likens to the Latin poet Horace. Despite this refinement and a distinct erudition, La Fontaine is also plainspoken, expressing himself with natural vigor and horse-sense (which is one reason why he is considered appropriate for young readers). But the mind behind these poems is as sophisticated as any in French poetry.

Paul Valéry recognized as much when he wrote in a preface to a reprint of La Fontaine's poem *Adonis:* "Let's note that an apparent nonchalance is in fact learned, relaxation is studied, and facility is the height of art . . . To my mind, such sustained art and purity exclude any laziness and any feeling of hail-fellow-well-met." This was a useful reply to the legend of a lackadaisical La Fontaine that began when Tallement called him a "great dreamer," citing instances of his absent-mindedness. In fact, La Fontaine was extremely productive, trying his hand at any project that might bring him some money, from plays and libretti—all failures—to a long poem about the then-trendy if unpromising subject of quinine.

Although hard-working, La Fontaine was also bent on pleasure, and notorious for paying little attention to traditional social mores. When he grew apart from his wife, whom he married when she was fourteen, he freely admitted it, saying that his wife's new lover "will tire of her just as I did." Yet he remained in communication with his spouse, sending her letters that reveal mutual understanding and complicity, which argues against some writers' totally negative view of their marriage. More accurate is the portrait of La Fontaine as an unconcerned father. In the Fables, he memorably expressed criticism of children's cruelty, and according to one anecdote, spent so little time with his son that he did not recognize him as an adult.

La Fontaine's personal philosophy, as reflected in his poetry, has been described as epicurean. In seventeenth-century France, authors like Pierre Gassendi wrote treatises on the neo-epicurean movement, which advocated enjoying today and not worrying about tomorrow. Other seventeenth-century poets, like Saint-Amant, also put the pleasure principle firmly to the fore. La Fontaine's poem "The Grasshopper and the Ant," contrasts a festive insect with a soberly industrious one, but not, as some readers may believe, as an argument for a blind work ethic. La Fontaine clearly saw himself as the improvident grasshopper, and the fate of receiving an unsympathetic reaction to his poverty may well have been based on personal experience, the wages of epicureanism. As Spitzer wrote, La Fontaine's "moral teaching is made to serve his aesthetic purpose," and not the reverse. A poem's purpose is its beauty and wit, not the moral it may offer. La Fontaine was a great poet and sensualist, a celebrator of life, and it is an odd destiny that makes him the bane of schoolchildren's homework in France today.

Some readers—those who erroneously class him as a children's author—are surprised that he also wrote racy books of Tales in verse, based on Boccaccio, Rabelais, and others. La Fontaine published his Fables only after his Tales had acquired notoriety, some think to defuse the spicy reputation the Tales had given him. Throughout his career, La Fontaine also made gestures toward piety, such as when he translated verse by St. Augustine. La Fontaine's interest in religious matters wavered throughout his life. On his deathbed, he was discovered to be wearing a cilice—usually mistranslated as "hair-shirt." The *Dictionnaire de l'Academie francaise* (1694) defines a cilice as a horse- or goat-hair belt, worn as a sign of penitence, rather than the full hair-shirts seen in biblical paintings. La Fontaine's religious beliefs were as inconstant as the rest of his will-o-the-wisp personality.

Religion and raciness coexisted in many writers of the time. The German author Picander (Christian Friedrich Henrici) published his text for J. S. Bach's *St. Matthew Passion* in a volume that also contained his erotic poems. As an author of bawdy material, La Fontaine was nevertheless sensible and cautious. The butts of his jokes were easy targets like lascivious monks and nuns, but unlike his sources such as Boccaccio or Poggio Bracciolini, he wrote no spoofs of homosexuality—perhaps from fear that these might be read as attacks on King Louis XIV's powerful and notoriously gay brother, Monsieur.

As he wrote in one fable, "Diversity is my motto." Any generalization about La Fontaine usually conceals a contradictory one. There are few more lovable and deeply human poets. All of these elements make him one of the most difficult of all to translate. English readers have been given a series of translations, including the poet and esthete Edward Marsh's (1931), but unlike other presentations of La Fontaine in English, the one by Marie Ponsot offers a choice of his Fables, Tales, and occasional verse. It is fine poetry in English, as well as being faithful to the original, because of the translator's rare combination of acute poetic skill and thorough knowledge of French. In 1963, when Marie Ponsot, then aged forty-two, was invited to contribute a volume of La Fontaine to the paperback Signet Classics series, she was known mainly as a translator of French books for children, including *The Golden Book of Fairy Tales*. Her small collection of poems, *True Minds*, had appeared in the City Lights poetry series in 1956, causing little comment. City Lights publisher Lawrence Ferlinghetti was a friend, but she had little in common with the most famous poets in that series, like Allen Ginsberg or Frank O'Hara. Not a Beat or free-verse experimentalist, Ponsot mastered form early on as a vehicle of emotion. Her main literary influences ranged from Shakespeare and Donne to James Joyce, H.D., and Djuna Barnes.

In the poet's personal life, her most urgent challenge in 1963 was raising her seven children. She worked on the La Fontaine project on and off for nearly three years. Around 1966, she also began a translation in rhyming couplets of the *Lais* of the medieval poet Marie de France. Sadly, she lost her drafts of this effort in Rattner's dairy restaurant in Manhattan. Unwilling to start over again since the results had not yet pleased her, and without a publisher's commission, Ponsot abandoned the Marie de France project. However much we may regret the loss of these translations, we can rejoice over the La Fontaine, even though its publication inspired no reviews at the time.

In the sixties, a new version of La Fontaine by a then-obscure poet might have been overlooked because of the comparative fame of Marianne Moore's version, published in 1954. Moore's renown as a distinguished American modernist concealed her own lack of mastery of French. In letters to a variety of experts, such as Harvard University's Harry Levin, Moore readily admitted her own limits. Her version is quintessentially more Moore than La Fontaine. In terms of American translations of other seventeenth century French verse, one of the few supreme contemporary precedents available to Ponsot was Richard Wilbur, whose splendid versions of Molière and Racine combine a mastery of French with an elegant command of English.

Ponsot's versions are very much her own, delightfully reflecting ways in which her own poetic preoccupations agree with La Fontaine's. Both poets radiate a sense of freedom within constraints, humor, and deep emotion. Ponsot's own writing goals—the antithesis of the Beat poets' "first thought, best thought" philosophy—have something in common with the original. She explains that in her own poems she uses a line that was "more like the French, with many more possible stressed and unstressed readings than most English metrics considers . . . There's a greater range of tonality in the French line than we are conscious of in English." This affinity doubtless aided her to faithfully follow the line lengths and rhyme schemes of the originals.

With this ideal in mind, she made draft translations of about half again as many poems as wound up in the final book, putting aside any that did not meet her strict standards. The result reveals an acute ear for the music of both languages. Accuracy, naturalness, and euphony combine for bewitching effects, such as these lines from "The Peacock Complains to Juno" (Fable II, 17):

"You, who flaunt the spectrum resplendent at your throat,
In a hundred silken shiftings of light and shade."

There are dancingly witty formulations, as in "The Frog Who Wanted to Make Herself Big as an Ox" (Fable I, 3):

"Princelings love protocol's punctilios . . ."

Compare this to the original: "*tout petit prince a des ambassadeurs*," which, if translated literally (every minor prince has his ambassadors), seems flat and dull. In addition to this high-flying mastery, there is also a gift for low comedy, which energizes "The Wolf Who Became a Shepherd" (Fable III, 3), with the gusto of a Tom and Jerry cartoon:

"The wolf's crook tripped him. He hit the ground;
The shepherd slew him with one blow.

All fakers slip up somewhere—a good thing to know.
    I've always said, and say so still,
    Wolves will be wolves, and so they will."

Poet and translator share an understanding of humanity, and of childhood activity. In "The Wolf, the Goat, and the Kid," (Fable IV, 14) Ponsot translates a password uttered by the goat ("*Foin du loup et de sa race!*"—literally "a fig for the wolf and his breed!") as:

"Wolf and wolves you stink stank stunk!"

Asked about this vivid formulation, Ponsot explains, "My kids would say to someone or to one another, 'You stink stank stunk.'" As in her translations of fairy tales, an adoption of childhood idiom gives extra resonance: "The Stag Who Saw His Reflection" (Fable VI, 9) contains the observation, "*Mes pieds ne me font point d'honneur*," which in English becomes lines that recall a counting game:

> "But he could hardly bear to look
> At his thin legs. 'Stick stick stick stick,
> Each stick with a wee tiny hoof . . . they make me sick!'"

Elsewhere, Ponsot reveals an ability to see things from a child's perspective. La Fontaine describes a tortoise as plodding along "like a senator," ("The Hare and The Tortoise", Fable VI, 10) which becomes:

> "She's like an old school principal.
> Pompously plugging on, dragging her feet."

Ponsot's range of reference is delightfully wide; in a single poem, "The Hare's Ears" (Fable V, 4) the tone varies from "and every last cerogerant" to "Poor dumb bunny." Far from bowdlerizing the French, on occasion she adds an extra bit of brass tacks, turning a phrase from "The Mountain in Labor" (Fable V, 10) about writers who emit "wind" (*du vent*) into:

> "They trumpet promises, but what's their work of art?
> A fart."

Incarnating Gallic humorousness, she even adds French-spirited jokes to the original, as in "The Snake and the File," (Fable V, 16) replacing a generic reference to watchmakers with a amusingly snooty remark about the Swiss, eternal pet peeve of the French:

> "Even the Swiss find snakes inauspicious neighbors."

The skill and power of a gifted poet able to work concisely in strict meter and rhyme is evident in "The Dog That Dropped His Prey for Its Shadow" (Fable VI, 17):

> . . . He fought, almost drowned, swam, endured,
> And staggered ashore having lost these three:
> A hope, a truth, a fantasy."

Drawing on memories of English-language culture, Ponsot discreetly paraphrases Bach's cantata "Sheep May Safely Graze" in "The Wolves and the Lambs" (Fable III, 13): ". . . grazers could not safely graze." She quotes John Keats's "wealth of globed peonies" in "The Vindicated Servant Girl" (Tale II,6) to evoke a headily erotic, poetically sensual narrative. And in an excerpt from "King Candule" (Tale IV, 8) she offers the line:

"Lusts laced his blood in arrowed rays"

suggesting how deeply this translator inhabits the original poetic idiom, creating faithful yet lovely lines in her own language. Sometimes the recreative spirit moves her to elaborate aptly amusing metaphors not in the original, such as the erotic symbolism of bell-clappers in "Smoked Eel" (Tale IV, 11):

"His valet had a wife as well,
A rather sweet one, honey-lipped;
The master, who was well-equipped,
Soon played the clapper to her bell
Until the valet chanced to see
Changes rung like a symphony
And called his tuneful wife away."

In terms of poetic influence, "Love and Folly," (Fable XII, 14) contains an echo of W. H. Auden's schoolmasterish responding to his own rhetorical questions:

"Aphrodite witnessed it.
Did she shriek her maternal grief? You know she did."

There are relatively few willful anachronisms, like "The Lion Holds Court" (Fable VII, 7), which describes taciturn "Normans or Vermonters." Or "The Lion, the Monkey, and the two Donkeys," (Fable XI, 5) with its updating of musical comparisons: "You're better than Stravinsky combined with Callas." For the most part, the poems in English inhabit the same universe as their originals, marking the identification between two poets.

Ponsot's own recent poem "Pourriture Noble" (from her collection *The Birdcatcher*) in which the invention of Château d'Yquem wine becomes a metaphor for the possible glories of old age, can be read as a kind of La Fontaine fable, complete with a final moral:

"Age is not
all dry rot.
It's never too late.
Sweet is your real estate."

Redeeming the sufferings of experience with artistry and wit, the conjunction of La Fontaine and Ponsot is a precious and rare example of verse translation. Widespread recognition of Ponsot's own poetic achievement began only in 1998, when she was awarded the National Book Critics Circle Award for *The Birdcatcher*. Increasingly, readers began to admire her metaphysic strength, complexity, and rigor, as well as stern beauty of language, illuminated by sharp rays of wit.

Scheduled for publication in 2002, her *Springing: New and Selected Poems* (Knopf) will include much unpublished work from the quarter-century between the publication of *True Minds* and her second collection, *Admit Impediment* (1981). During these years dedicated to raising her children, although Ponsot published nothing apart from a few scattered appearances in *Poetry* magazine, she did keep writing. Her La Fontaine is her most significant public manifestation during these years, and proves a lasting pleasure for readers.

—Benjamin Ivry

Further Reading on La Fontaine

IN ENGLISH:

Marsh, Edward, (tr.), *The fables of Jean de La Fontaine*, London: W. Heinemann, Ltd., 1931.

Spitzer, Leo, "The Art of Transition in La Fontaine," in *Essays on Seventeenth Century French Literature*, (tr. and ed. David Bellos), New York: Cambridge University Press, 1983.

Sweetser, Marie-Odile, *La Fontaine*, Boston: Twayne, 1985.

Wadsworth, Philip A., *Young La Fontaine*, Evanston: Northwestern University Press, 1952.

IN FRENCH:

Bared, Robert, *La Fontaine*, Paris: Seuil: Ecrivains du toujours, 1995.

Clarac, Pierre, *La Fontaine par lui-meme*. Paris: Seuil, 1961.

La Fontaine, l'homme et l'oeuvre, Paris: Hatier, 1969.

Collinet, Jean-Pierre, ed., *La Fontaine, Fables, contes et nouvelles*, Paris: Gallimard, Bibliotheque de la Pleiade, 1991.

Dandrey, Patrick, *La Fontaine ou les metamorphoses d'Orphee*, Paris: Gallimard-Decouvertes, 1995

Duchene, Roger, *Jean de la Fontaine*, Paris: Fayard, 1995.

Fumaroli, Marc, ed., *La Fontaine, Fables*, Paris: Imprimerie Nationale, 2 vol., 1985.

Le poète et le roi: Jean de La Fontaine en son siecle, Paris: Editions de Fallois, 1997.

Gassendi, Pierre, "Traité de la philosophie d'Epicure, IIIe partie: l'éthique ou la morale" in *Libertins du XVIIe siècle*, Jacques Prévot, Thierry Bedouelle, and Etienne Wolff. eds., Paris: Gallimard, Bibliothèque de la Pléiade, 1998.

TRANSLATOR'S PREFACE

In establishing the contents of this collection, I kept several aims in mind. I wanted to include the famous classics from among the fables; I wanted to show the scope of La Fontaine's observant wit, and the steady growth of his skill in choosing material and in extracting the unexpected as well as the obvious from it; I also wanted to provide some of those passages that tell us, as no biography can, how he felt about his own time and work. These general aims governed my selection only to a point. Beyond it were two determining notions: the constancy of my own pleasure in the French poem; and the hope that my translation had not entirely betrayed it.

The twelve books of fables are justly so famous in their own right that it is hard to choose from among them. It is not made easier by an historical circumstance unlike any in English literature: since much of the French school curriculum has been relatively static since Napoleon, the fables have been the constant fare of generations of children. To call "classic" a work that has withstood erosion by time is—if inadequate—useful and not inaccurate; yet in ascertaining which are the "classic" fables, this criterion lacks its usual validity. Their resistance to time has been affected by an aura—like that about *"Gallia est omnes divisa in partes tres,"* surely not Caesar's grandest line—engendered by the efforts of countless schoolboys. At any rate, familiarity with La Fontaine's fables—a joy in itself—also means familiarity with a denominator common to many generations of Frenchmen; all readers and writers have been touched by them.

The *Contes* (tales), more plainly unsuited to early childhood education, bulk large in La Fontaine's total work and were very popular in his day; they seem less widely read now. (I have not seen English versions.) In them La Fontaine is very much as he saw himself—worldly, clever, and knowingly entertaining. They tell a good deal about their author and his audience; and in the original they are wonderfully funny. I wanted to reproduce at least that relish with which La Fontaine sidestepped vulgar language while telling a vulgar story.

Whatever their excellence—and they easily surpass his dramatic pieces and occasional verse—the droll tales fall short of the deft perfection La Fontaine exhibits in the fables, which were his major pursuit.

Centuries of fabulists had already used the materials, in Persian, Greek, Latin, and Anglo-Norman as well as in French. The plots had been made firm and tight, the action streamlined, the characters personalized, the morals drawn. Renditions in late Latin, ponied and annotated, were common texts for schoolboys' translation, so integral a part of the prevalent culture were they.

The language into which—and by which—they were formed when La Fontaine worked with it was an unusual instrument. The Acadèmie was established in 1635 to "purify" French according to "discipline" and "reason" and the status quo. It had not yet had time to produce the deep freeze that paralyzed the substrata of French verse in the eighteenth and nineteenth centuries. It had arrested the pell-mell process of linguistic growth and accretion—but just long enough previous to La Fontaine's work for the structure and meaning of the language to have emerged with beauty and clarity and freshness.

La Fontaine had, then, his two major ingredients, language and subject, at hand. He had the further advantage of writing for a specific audience that was well known to him. But there is a saying that neither the raw materials nor the diners make great cuisine: for that, you need genius in the cook.

La Fontaine had the genius, and has delighted the tastes of every generation since his. These versions of his fables and tales use the same rhyme schemes, the same number of lines, and the same number of syllables per line as the originals. I trust they do not stray any great distance from the original sense or spirit, though they must do without the sheen, the "certain radiance" of surface, the ear-delighting absolute felicity of La Fontaine. These are his most particular and therefore his least imitable gifts.

The French text used for these translations is:

La Fontaine (Jean de.) *Fables, Contes, et Nouvelles*; texte établi et annoté par René Groos (*Fables*) et par Jacques Schiffrin (*Contes*); préface d'Edmond Pilon et René Groos. (Bibliothèque de la Pléiade) Gallimard, Paris, 1959, Volume I.
    Oeuvres Diverses; texte établi et annoté par Pierre Clarac. (Bibliothèque de la Pléiade) Gallimard, Paris, 1958. Volume II; revised with important additions from the first edition of 1942.

It is not only easily available, but a work of scholarly summation in a field long populous with laborers. It offers a bibliography for the *Fables*, the *Contes*, and the *Oeuvres complètes* in Volume I; and a selected bibliography of writings on La Fontaine's life and works in Volume II.

—Marie Ponsot

"The Peacock Complains to Juno" (Book II, 17)

DEDICATION OF THE FABLES

To my Lord the Dauphin
My Lord:
   If anything in the world of letters be ingenious, it is the manner in which Aesop presents a moral. It would have been most desirable to have had hands other than mine add poetic grace to his work, which the very wisest of the ancient sages judged to have its usefulness. I make bold, my Lord, to present these my few attempts to you. The encounter is one suited to these, your early years. You are at the age when amusement and games are permitted to princes, while at the same time you are certainly devoting some of your thoughts to serious reflections. Both elements meet in the fables we owe to Aesop. Though they may seem childish, I confess, that childishness serves to envelop some important truths. I do not doubt, my Lord, that you will look favorably on work at once useful and agreeable: what can be better than these two qualities, which are at the root of human knowledge. Aesop's art is unique in that he joined the one to the other. When his work is read, the seeds of virtue are subtly sown in the heart; the heart is taught to know itself without heeding what it studies, and while under the impression it is quite differently occupied. He whom His Majesty has chosen to instruct you has happily employed this adroit method. He uses it so that you may learn without pain, indeed frankly with pleasure, whatever a prince needs to know. We expect a great deal from this conduct. There are, however, other considerations from which we expect infinitely more. Those are, my Lord, the qualities that our invincible monarch gave you from your birth; and the example that he provides

for you every day. When you see him shaping such great plans; when you think of him who beholds without flinching the agitation of Europe and the machinations intended to turn him from his enterprise; when on his first attempt he penetrates right to the heart of a province where every step presents insurmountable barriers, and then he subjugates another province in one week, during the season most inimical to war, when in the hearts of other princes rest and pleasure hold sway; when not content to dominate men, he decides he will also triumph over the elements; and when on his return from an expedition where he triumphed like an Alexander you see him reign over his peoples like an Augustus: you will certify how true it is, my Lord, that you sigh after glory as does he, despite the years that separate you from it; you wait impatiently for the time when you can rival him in love of that divine mistress. You do not merely wait, my Lord; you hasten the day. Proof of this is in the noble restlessness, the liveliness, the warmth, the marks of spirit and courage and greatness of soul, which you evidence at all times. It is certainly a source of real joy to our monarch; it is moreover a sight pleasurable to the whole universe to see such growth in the young sapling that will one day cover so many peoples and nations with its shade. I should expand this theme, but since the plan I have made to amuse you is better proportioned to my strength than is that of praising you, I come quickly to the fables, and shall add to the truths I have already stated only this one: that is, my Lord, that I am with respectful zeal, your very humble, very obedient, and very faithful servant,

De La Fontaine.

FABLES

"The Fox and the Stork" (Book I, 18)

First and Second Parts

BOOK I

I

The Grasshopper and the Ant
(LA CIGALE ET LA FOURMI)

The grasshopper sang her song
    Summer long.
When the winter chilled the woods
She had stored no worldly goods,
Not a scrap or bit or wing,
Grub or gnat or anything.
She begged Ant, her rich neighbor
Whose wealth came from hard labor,
For just enough nourishment
To keep her till winter went.
"What you lend I shall pay back
Plus interest, in a new sack,
Well before midsummer's growth—
Gracious Insect, I take oath!"
If ants have faults, least of these
Is to lend without reason.
"What did you do last season?"
Ant asked. "I sang with the breeze,
Sang by choice and sang by chance,

Please ma'am, as grasshoppers do."
"As they do. How nice for you.
You sang," said Ant. "Now go dance!"

2
The Crow and the Fox
(LE CORBEAU ET LE RENARD)

A crow with a prize cheese clapped in his beak
 Perched high beyond reach or reproach.
The scent drew Fox who decided to speak
 Using more or less this approach:
 "Sir Crow! A pleasure to behold!
I love that plumage, neat, restrained, yet—glistening, bold!
 On my word, if your singing voice
 Shows a tastefulness half as choice
You are the phoenix king of our community."
Crow, flattered foolish, opened his beak and sang free
 Although not with impunity.
The cheese fell to Fox who said, "My poor friend, thank me
For my demonstration of a truth you should learn.
 Flattery always serves the turn
 Of the flatterer; you pay for his pranks.
The lesson is: Don't listen. The cheese is mine; thanks."
 Crow shrank in shame, and murmured "I
Paid too much to learn too late how flatterers lie."

3
The Frog Who Wanted to Make Herself Big as an Ox
(LA GRENOUILLE QUI VEUT SE FAIRE AUSSI GROSSE QUE LE BOEUF)

A frog saw an ox and was stirred
    To admiration for his size.
She, no bigger than the egg of a mockingbird,
Began to stretch, and puff up, to hyperbolize
    Herself to oxen dimensions, crying,
       "Watch, great friend! Shall I keep trying?
Look!" she puffed, "Have I already reached your size?"
       "No."
"Now see!" "Still no." "How's this?" "No closer than at first,"
Said the ox. The ambitious diminutive so
    Outdid herself then that she burst.
In liking to seem grand, most men are no sages.
Middle-class folk live in imitation châteaux;
    Princelings love protocol's punctilios,
       And minor knights must have pages.

4
Two Mules
(LES DEUX MULETS)

A mule, his pack heavy with oats, met on the road
    A mule who bore tax receipts in his pack
And gloried in the honor conferred on his back
By the value of his splendid if heavy load.
       Smartly down the highway he strode
       And kept his bells atinkle all the way.
       Fear came riding out of the sun.

The internal revenue one
Was reined in hard by robbers. He kicked in dismay
         Until they forced him to obey.
         He fell when the robbers had done,
Brought low by wounds, moaning and groaning wearily.
"Is this the thanks I was led to expect?" he sighed.
"While the farm mule walks away from the fight scot free,
         I lie in mortal misery."
         He heard, "I am a burden's beast;
Your high-class job has trouble as a dividend.
Were you a menial laborer like me, my friend,
         You'd still have your health, at least."

6
_____

The Heifer, the Goat, and the Lamb, Together with the Lion

(LA GÉNISSE, LA CHÈVRE, ET LA BREBIS, EN SOCIÉTÉ AVEC LE LION)

Heifer, Goat, and their small sister Lamb were the friends
Of Lion, overlord of the vicinity.
This social group of long ago had as its ends
Common goods and needs which gave them affinity.
Once, Lady Goat sent word there would be dividends
From a stag just caught near the lakes of her domain.
They foregatherd, and Lion counted on his claws,
"One, two, three, four: split the stag in four; that is plain."
He did so, making the best quarter his, "Because
You gladly honor kings; right, Heifer? right, Goat?
And who's a king? a king is a lion; right, Lamb?
         Lion's my name, king's who I am,
         Right?" They accorded him their vote.
"The second quarter belongs to the strongest one,
Me . . . Unless . . . would someone like to try to win it?
No? Now the third. The bravest gets that. What's his name?
Why, me! And the fourth; if any one states her claim,
         I'll kill her in one flat minute."

9
The City Rat and the Country Rat

(LE RAT DE VILLE ET LE RAT DES CHAMPS)

City Rat once engineered
A dinner for his cousin,
Country Rat. The meal appeared
In courses by the dozen.

They sat at a Chinese rug
And porcelain was their dish;
You can tell they were as snug
As any lordlings might wish.

The dinner was rich and rare
Composed of well-made delights,
But a sudden someone there
Scared away their appetites.

Close to the door there was an
Awfully intrusive sound;
City Rat, Country Cousin
Vanished at a single bound.

Then the footsteps died away;
The rats returned to the floor.
City Rat said, "Cousin, pray
Serve yourself a trifle more."

Country Rat said, "Not now, sir.
Next time you come see me.
I intend to cast no slur
On city hospitality—

But I like peace when I sit,
Home, the calm is measureless.
I find this life pleasureless
Now that fear has nibbled it."

13

The Thieves and the Donkey

(LES VOLEURS ET L'ANE)

Two thieves stole a donkey. "Keep it!" one insisted.
The other wanted to sell. They argued it out
      With blows, hot and heavy-fisted;
Forgetting the donkey, they plunged into their bout.
      A third thief came along, alone,
      And took the donkey for his own.

The donkey is like a small, powerless nation
      That tempts the lords of creation
—Georgians, let us say, or Tartars, or the Chinese.
      (Notice I've named not two but three of these;
      Aggressors are always in good supply.)
They seize on lands not rightly theirs, then treatify.
But before they sign a fourth thief hops on the throne
      And gets the donkey for his own.

18

The Fox and the Stork

(LE RENARD ET LA CICOGNE)

Fox rejoiced. He had found a way to ask Miss Stork
To dine with him on a new economy plan.
He boiled a poor soup from leftover bones of pork
      Then—friend Fox is no gentleman—
Poured it over the bottom of his flattest dish.
Miss Stork ate nothing; her long beak was no spoon-bill.
As he lapped, she said, "Dear Fox, I hope you soon will
Come and dine with me—next Saturday, if you wish."
      She smiled. He licked his dish clean and yapped,
        "Good of you!
Saturday? I'll come. I'll be happy to."

A greedy miser's dream comes true
     When food is free; with that in view
   Fox went eagerly to the rendezvous.
      He praised Miss Stork, her charm, her grace,
      Her taste in furnishing the place.
      He said, "I smell, if I am right,
The kind of cooking that by right
Is fit for kings—something sauté, in a rich sauce."
She nodded; he grinned—until Miss Stork served the course
      Far down a long-necked, small-mouthed vase
Well suited to her beak but impossibly thin
For Fox's stubby muzzle. Under her cool gaze
He left, his hunger intact but minus his grin.
Too ashamed to complain, he sought his lonely hole,
Embarrassed as would be a fox a chicken stole,
His tail tucked in, his ears disconsolate.
    Tricksters: swallow this fable whole.
    It's you your tricks humiliate.

20

The Rooster and the Pearl
(LE COQ ET LA PERLE)

Once a pecking rooster found
A fine pearl. He took it round
To the nearest jewelry store.
"They call this priceless; for me
One golden wheat grain," said he,
"If my own, would please me more."
A fool was willed a rare bound
Manuscript. He took it round
To the first bookshop he saw.
"It's good, I guess," he said. "Still
The words on one one-dollar bill
Of my own, would please me more."

BOOK II

3

The Wolf Pleads Against the Fox Before the Monkey
(LE LOUP PLAIDANT CONTRE LE RENARD PAR-DEVANT LE SINGE)

A wolf, claiming theft, caused a sensation
By refusing lawyers and summoning to court
His neighbor, a fox of tarnished reputation.
    A monkey judge (no relation
To judges you know) sat and listened as they fought.
    He heard a vast compilation
Of amateur unlawyered prevarication;
The attacks and counterclaims were beyond belief.
    Every fresh recrimination
    Made him pray for peroration.
    His sentence said, "Thief versus thief,
Both guilty! Both will pay court costs in this attack
    Plus twice the legal penalty.
You, Wolf, never lost what you have sued to get back.
Fox, you steal that much—though not from Wolf—constantly.
Right or wrong, this verdict leaves justice least undone
By condemning two criminals instead of one."

4
The Two Bulls and a Frog
(LES DEUX TAUREAUX ET UNE GRENOUILLE)

Two bulls fought to win a heifer and rule the herd.
    A frog in an algae-green pond
    Sighed. Another snapped, "You're absurd!
    This isn't the Slough of Despond!"
    The first discreetly sighed aside.
    And croaked, "Trouble's coming. You'll see.
    The losing bull will have to flee
From the flowered fields where herd and heifer reside.
The winner will rule the kingdom of the meadow grass;
The loser takes what's left, the marsh—and us, alas.
There'll be snapped stalks where once reeds towered tall and
        brown.
There'll be death beneath hooves that will trample us down
Carelessly, constantly. We'll pay in blood and fright
No matter who wins the herd and heifer tonight."
    The prophecy was good though harsh.
    One bull had nowhere else to stay
    So he came to claim the green marsh
    And squashed a hundred frogs a day.
    Whoever wins—I sadly state—
Lesser folk always pay for the wars of the great.

6
The Bird Struck by an Arrow
(L'OISEAU BLESSÉ D'UNE FLÈCHE)

Near death, stricken by a swift bright-feathered arrow,
Grieving to see his life's room so soon grow narrow,
A bird sang out in a dark upsurge of sorrow,

"You are twice cruel who use us to hurt us, who borrow
        Our feathers for your fatal arrows' speed;
Our own flight follows our flight; we both strike and bleed,
Sons of Japheth! Know yourselves and learn to lament!
You find my death ironic? Think before you laugh:
Half of you live to furnish, with vicious intent,
        Armaments to the other half."

II

The Lion and the Rat
(LE LION ET LE RAT)

Do what you can to please those you meet; understand
That even the strongest may need even the weak.
Here are two samples—there are many I might seek—
        From the abundant proofs on hand.
        A rat taking the air, emerged
To discover he stood between a lion's claws.
The King of Beasts, for once by kingly mercy urged,
Let Rat go, grateful although shaking on his paws.
        The good deed was not done in vain.
        Isn't it nonsense to maintain
        A rat might save a lion's skin?
Yet this lion, when pacing his kingdom's frontier,
        Fell in a net and roared with fear.
Since roars do not rip nets, he stayed roaring therein.
Rat ran to the rescue and chewed with devotion
Till the net raveled off in a ruin, all loose.
        Time and patience are of more use
        Than force or fierce emotion.

12

The Dove and the Ant
(LA COLOMBE ET LA FOURMI)

This tale gives examples of smaller friends in need,
Ant leaned out too far over a stream; she fell down
And spat and floundered wetly knowing she would drown,
Until Dove charitably thrust out a long weed
Under Ant's claws to bridge the water's broad expanse,
And Ant ambled back across it to safety.
Well, Dove had acted out of simple charity
With no thought of reward. But just then by some chance
  A barefoot farm boy happened by,
Hunting, bow strung and arrows ready to let fly.
He was looking for game, something harmless to slay.
  Love's gentle bird caught his eye;
He could almost smell it baking, thinking, "Hooray!
Pot pie for dinner—the perfect end of a day."
  Ant stung his foot with all her might.
  He shook it, chasing her away
And warning Dove, who took refuge in sudden flight.
The farm boy's dream of dinner flew as the dove fled
  And pot pie was replaced by bread.

17

The Peacock Complains to Juno*
(LE PAON SE PLAIGNANT À JUNON)

  Juno's peacock pouted as he cried
"Why must you be unjust to me? I've tried and tried
  But still they all laugh when I speak.
  Great goddess, why did you provide
  A throat like mine with such a shriek?

When that drab little nightingale opens her beak
   A flood of glory turns all season into spring,
      Yet I—a peacock!—cannot sing."
      Juno raged. "Bird nature, bird wit!
    Jealous, and meanly unashamed of it!
You covet the dulcet nightingale's poignant note—
You, who flaunt the spectrum resplendent at your throat
In a hundred silken shiftings of light and shade
     As arched and crested you parade
With fantail intricately trembling in the light!
    Why, beside you, all birds are plain.
    What bird alive can claim the right
     To every gift? None. I ordain
For each creature a particular perfection
(Whence the privilege of taste, the play of dilection).
Some are born strong as a king, some strong as a slave;
Falcons are slight and lightning-swift; eagles are brave;
    Crows are prophets; their croak is grave;
Ravens warn . . . and they all praise their lot; none complain.
    Craven peacock, how dare you crave
More than you have! Silence! or I shall pluck you plain;
    Unplumed, you might learn to behave."

*Juno, a Roman goddess who presided over marriage and childbirth; in another guise, as the Greek goddess Hera, she placed the many eyes of the herdsman Argus on the tail feathers of her sacred bird, the peacock.

BOOK III

3
The Wolf Who Became a Shepherd
(LE LOUP DEVENU BERGER)

A wolf, logical and lamb-loving, saw sheep flee
    When he came near. "They think they're wise!"
He growled. "All right for them! I'm not so dumb. They'll see!
    I'll get me a perfect disguise."
He shouldered a shepherd's hide shirt which hid his tail,
    Made a stick his crook, played the scale
    On Pan-pipes, conscientiously;
    Thought, and longed for literacy.
He'd have liked a sign stuck on his hat, plain to see,
"I'm Shepherd Joe. The Shepherd of this Flock is Me."
    Proud in his costume, standing tall
With forepaws braced on his crook so as not to fall,
Wolf Joe the Joker neared the flock of sleeping sheep.
The real Shepherd Joe slept too—crook, pipes, dog and all.
    The costumed joker let them sleep.
He thought, "I'm not greedy. Two sheep—or three, if small—
Are all I want. Besides, big surpluses don't keep."
    Planning menus, he thought, enthralled,
"If they were closer, I'd choose some, while I'm waiting;
Shepherds call sheep, I'm sure they do." So, creating
    The role within himself, Wolf called,
    And was absolutely appalled.
The sounds he had made were not sheep-captivating,
Not shepherdly, but wolf-howls so devastating
    To his disguise that his act stalled.

The place rang with life and sound,
Up leaped the shepherd's angry hound,
The sheep, and Shepherd Joe.
The wolf's crook tripped him. He hit the ground;
The shepherd slew him with one blow.

All fakers slip up somewhere—a good thing to know.
I've always said, and say so still,
Wolves will be wolves, and so they will.

9

The Wolf and the Stork
(LE LOUP ET LA CICOGNE)

A wolf was devouring a feast,
Gobbling fast, the way wolves do it,
When he choked; his breathing all but ceased;
He feared he'd never live through it.
There was a bone lodged in his throat too deep to reach.
Luckily—for he had lost the power of speech—
Mrs. Stork saw his frantic wave
And put her natural fear aside.
She came courageously to look, and stayed to save.
Surgically neat, she got the bone, then asked with pride
For some token of gratitude.
"You," he howled, "have a head on you
As token, fool! What fortitude
I showed, not biting your neck through,
And it down my throat! What kinder thing could I do?
Get out, and stay out of my way.
Next time we meet, you'll rue the day!"

10

The Lion Slain by a Man

(LE LION ABATTU PAR L'HOMME)

A painting on exhibition
Showed an unarmed man who had slain
A big lion in prime condition.
It put man's supremacy plain;
Man looked, and bloomed with borrowed pride.
A lion passed and saw, and snorted with disdain.
    "Quite!" he said. "The lion lies slain
By poetic license. . . . It's snide,
But legal; a trick, an excuse
To reconcile men to their race.
We lions would tell the proud truth, had we the use
    Of oils to paint it in men's place."

11

The Fox and the Grapes

(LE RENARD ET LES RAISINS)

A fox (born, I suppose, in Maine-like Normandy)
Saw ripe-seeming grapes high on a trellis-trained vine.
    Half starved, he stared up hungrily
    At the plump bronzed bunch, rich with wine.
They would have made a Lupercalian meal
    But hung beyond his attaining,
So he said, "Sour grapes! Fit for peasants! I'm genteel."
    Wasn't that wiser than complaining?

12

The Swan and the Cook
(LE CYGNE ET LE CUISINIER)

With the birds who made merry
In a rich man's aviary
Were a gosling and a swan:
The latter to enchant the man whose grounds he graced,
The former, Swan's young friend Goose, strictly for his taste,
Since he was cook's charge. Two white birds in unison,
They shared the mansion's sunny, lilied lake, and there
They sported together, now swimming side by side,
Now plunged under water, now rising, wings spread wide,
Without exhausting the pleasures of open air.
One day the cook had looked too long on wine too red;
He took Swan for Goose, and having prepared spiced bread,
Planned to stuff the Swan for dinner. Poor Swan, resigned,
Murmured his swan song, though his throat was sore confined.
    The cook was terribly shaken
    To find himself mistaken.
"I never meant to stuff such a grand singer, no!
May no ax of mine give such a voice its death blow!
    Only criminals would cut a throat of such charm."

Amid life's accidents it may be well to know
    Soft answers can keep us from harm.

13

The Wolves and the Lambs

(LES LOUPS ET LES BREBIS)

After more than a thousand years of active war
The wolves sought a peace pact with the sheep. It was clear
Both sides would benefit, could both sides cast out fear.
Wolves often dined on sheep, but to even the score
Many a shepherd sported wolf-hide clothes and gear.
Neither side was free; grazers could not safely graze
     Nor slayers slay the grazing strays;
Fear spoils the natural joys, even of food and sleep.
So peace was declared; they exchanged, with pride and praise,
Their hostages: lambs went to wolves, wolf cubs to sheep.
The standard rituals of truce were carried out.
     Peace dawned—and would have reigned, no doubt,
If cubs could be kept cubs. But wolves from wolf cubs grow,
True to kind: the young wolves' rage to kill grew strong;
They waited. One day the shepherds left, not for long,
     Long enough for the young wolves, though,
To liberate their adolescent libido.
They killed the plumpest of the lambs and carried them
In triumph to the woods where the wolf pack waited.
The dogs, found fast asleep, were left immolated;
     Poor beasts, they had overrated
The trust due unenforced peace pacts. Their requiem
Might have as theme that no true peace-seeker permits
     False innocence to fog his wits.
Mere shocked protests won't stop wars. Real trust is complex,
     Peace is loved by all men, yes—
     But lost unless conscious strength checks
     All men's lust, rage and wantonness.

14

The Lion Who Had Grown Old

(LE LION DEVENU VIEUX)

The lion, dreaded and dreadnought,
Grew old and mourned the majesty he'd known so long.
At the last his own subjects hunted him for sport;
    To know him so weak made them feel strong.
Even the horse got close enough to land a kick.
The wolf's teeth gashed, the bull's horn gouged his ancient hide.
He lay too weak to roar, friendless and unallied,
Humbled by time, ashamed and sick,
And waited for the end without complaint—at least
Until he saw the ass intended to attack.
He groaned, "Die I must, but your straw breaks my back.
It doubles death to suffer it from such a beast."

15

Philomel and Procne*

(PHILOMÈLE ET PROGNÉ)

Procne the Swallow soared one day
    And flew far from her city nest
    Until she reached the sylvan rest
Where her sister, Philomel Nightingale, held sway.
On arrival she chatted. "How are you, dear?
It's frightfully long since we had your last visit—
Not since Thrace, not less than a thousand years, is it?
Tell me all about it: what do you do all year?
    For the future—what do you plan?
Why not quit this solitude as soon as you can!"
Said Philomel, "Nowhere is lovelier than here."
"But your voice!" her sister cried. "It's going to waste

Among wild beasts and earless trees
And a few peasants with no taste.
It's your duty to use your gift. Do as you please,
But you should come to the city and share your song.
Then too, forests bring back, I'm sure,
The dreadful anguish Tereus made you endure
In woods like these when—wild and wrong!—
He exposed all your beauty to his fierce attack."
"It is because his bitter memory still burns,"
She replied, "that cities do not beckon me back.
When I see how men act, alack!
The thought of that outrage returns."

In Shakespeare's play Titus Andronicus, *a lovely Athenian princess, was raped and mutilated by the Thracian king Tereus. In revenge, she and her sister Procne fed the king a dish containing the cooked remains of his son Itys. To save them from Tereus's wrath, the gods changed Procne into a nightingale and Philomel into a swallow (or in the Latin version that La Fontaine followed, the reverse). As for Tereus, he was changed into a hoopoe.*

16

The Drowned Woman
(LA FEMME NOYÉE)

I'm not like those who can say, "She's drowned? That's not much—
A woman, who is beastly dead."
It is much indeed, I insist; women are such
That we must mourn their loss; by them our joy is fed.
Let that statement preface my next tale of a wife
Taken where the river ran swift
And borne to the end of her life.
Her husband sought the corpse, trailing the river's drift,
So that he might at least provide
Burial for her mortal clay
In the usual decent way.

Two strangers walked the riverside
        Not knowing what had happened there.
The husband asked if they had noticed any trace
        In the water or any place
Of his wife. "None," said one. "But look downstream; go where
The river leads you." The other laughed. "Don't do that!
        I'd turn and try the other way,
Against the stream, if I were in your position.
        However the river may stray,
No matter how strong its natural bent has been,
        A woman's will is hard to bend;
        Her need to contradict will win;
        She'll go against the current, friend."
The man had chosen an ill time to joke and grin.
        I don't know if contrariness
        Must or must not be feminine,
        Is or is not a genuine
        Inborn female trait; but I guess
        It grows into an addiction.
        Persons born with that affliction
        Of passion for contradiction
        Keep it, till their valediction.

17

The Weasel in the Attic Storeroom
(LA BELETTE ENTRÉE DANS UN GRENIER)

Supple Miss Weasel, convalescent, slinked right in
Through a narrow hole, to an attic storage bin;
        A long illness left her glad
        To rest there where much food was stored.
        Since her small bones were still ill-clad,
        What stout feasts the gallant girl had,
Lunching from dawn to dark and dining till she snored.

So she, when her health was restored,
Waxed fat; in this case that was sad.
She had spent some days without a hungry second
When she heard a sound outside; the great world beckoned.
She nosed the hole, and cried, "Is this where I came in?"
She searched, returned, and cried again,
With a surprise both woebegone and genuine,
"I did come in here. But the hole was bigger then!"
A rat, observing her dismay,
Said, "You had a flat belly when you came this way.
Empty you came; empty you must go. . . . I refer
To no real person, live or dead; I'm not stealthy;
I'm talking to Miss Weasel and only to her;
Her ill-got gains are unhealthy."

BOOK IV

5

The Donkey and the Little Dog
(L'ANE ET LE PETIT CHIEN)

Talent has limits that if passed
Deprive our every act of grace.
In roles that want wit, gilt, and lace
Bumbling farmboys are miscast.
Rare is the man in whom every gift is innate.
Talent and charm, of course, are not commensurate.
No one is to everyone's taste—
As we know from the donkey who met disaster
While trying to charm his master.
His motive was good but his tactics were misplaced.
He observed, "A dog's life is great!
Our owners like dog-tricks so well
They treat her like a demoiselle,
And yet they never hesitate
To beat me to a fare-thee-well.
She puts up a paw and gets kisses.
That's a thing anyone might do.
It works, too. I've watched her act; it never misses.
It's high time I tried that trick too."
The next time he saw his owner
He clopped clumsily up and, giving a grand grin,
Made his blunt corned hoof the donor
Of a most affectionate hard right to the chin
Accompanied by brays, a serenade of din.

"Ouch, my ears!" yelled his owner, staggering upright;
"Ouch, my chin! I think it's broken, you blasted blight!
Hey, there, groom, get this creature out of here at once.
See if you can beat manners into the poor dunce."
      There's the story, all told, all right.

8

The Man and the Wooden Idol
(L'HOMME ET L'IDOLE DE BOIS)

A certain pagan cherished a god made of wood.
It was one of those gods that have ears and hear not,
Yet the pagan hoped miracles would be his lot
      And spent on it all that he could:
      Burnt offerings, lustrations, vows,
Bulls sacrificed with flower garlands on their brows.
      No idol in history had
      A richer, more varied diet.
Despite such worship, the idol did not once add
To his owner's wealth, good luck, or household quiet.
Worse, every time that storm or trouble struck somewhere
      And receipts fell off, as they may,
The man felt the blow, and his purse suffered its share;
But he still had the idol's same upkeep to pay.
Sick of getting nothing while giving much, at last
He took a crowbar, smashed the thing, and in it saw
Pounds of gold. "When I did well by you in the past
You never dropped even a penny from your maw!
Go find other altars. Out of my house with you!
      The way you act is nothing new.
      A fool like you is, as I've learned,
Useless without his master's stick across his back.
The more kindness I showed you, the less you returned.
      I was right to try a new tack."

9

The Crow Dressed in Peacock Feathers

(LE GEAI PARÉ DES PLUMES DU PAON)

A peacock cast its feathers. A passing crow saw,
 And stuck them in among his own;
He swore their cock-eyed glory was home-grown,
 And walked out grand from crup to caw.
Real peacocks looked twice, and shrieking at his deceit
 Pecked, plucked, beaked until in defeat
He sought his own. The crows, shocked by his wild, wrecked state,
Thought him a foreigner and forced him to retreat.
 Some peacock crows circulate
On two feet, decked out in cast-offs of others' brains;
They are known as plagiarists by these ill-got gains.
 Enough said. I do not design
To cause these people any further harm or pains.
 Theirs is no business of mine.

10

The Camel and the Driftwood

(LE CHAMEAU ET LES BÂTONS FLOTTANTS)

The first man who saw camels fled;
 The second man stopped short, instead,
Then approached them; the third thought it ordinary
 To bridle a dromedary.
Time makes the strange and rare as familiar as bread.
What strikes us at first sight as terrible, we dread
 Until mere daily ritual
 Has made the sight habitual.
That reminds me: there's a sea-watch I might mention.
 It was kept in times of tension.
Sighting a dim, distant form, vast in dimension,

They cried, "Warships! sound the alarm!"
And, "Heaven keep our cause from harm!"
Then they looked again, and said they'd seen a slow boat . . .
No, a sailboat . . . no, a rowboat . . .
What they had sighted was driftwood.
For some, a suitable gift would
Be the moral of this story:
Given distance, any trifle takes on glory.

14

The Fox and the Portrait Head
(LE RENARD ET LE BUSTE)

Grecian actors wore masks—and so do most great men.
Fools are impressed by any gaudy specimen;
A donkey will judge by what stands before his eyes.
A fox, however, insists that he must first know;
He sees all angles shrewdly, and should he surmise
A fine facade is just for show,
He will quote (although modest about fox culture)
A fox anecdote on sculpture:
A fox saw a hollow hero's bust, twice life size.
Knowing where the line between art and subject lies,
"A splendid head," he sighed. "Pity it has no brain."
Many famous figures are, like that bust, inane.

15

The Wolf, the Goat, and the Kid
(LE LOUP, LA CHÈVRE, ET LE CHEVREAU)

A mother goat's milk grew scant, so she went to browse
In the pasture with the cows.
But first, door locked and key hid,

She instructed her young kid.
"Mind, whoever may appear
Keep the door shut till you hear
The watchword just as I bid:
'Wolf and wolves you stink stank stunk!'"
She was just saying that phrase
When wolf passed, heard, and slunk
Quickly away from her gaze,
Behind trees where he could scan
The house, learn the phrase, and plan.
She left without suspicion.
Seeing his chance, he fared forth to gain admission.
        In a nanny-goat bawl
He cried, knocking, "Wolf or wolves, you stink," and so on,
        Thinking that with that to go on
The kid would let him in. Instead, hearing the call,
He bent to the keyhole and cried, "Show your white foot!"
(Few wolves' feet are white—though some do call sneaks
        Lightfoot.)
Taken aback to find the kid quite unafraid,
The wolf went home and abandoned the masquerade.
What would have become of the kid had he relied
On one verbal shield to defend his tender hide,
        When by pure chance the wolf had won
        Access to its every letter?
        Two safeguards are better than one;
The more protective measures we take, the better.

17

A Saying of Socrates

(PAROLE DE SOCRATE)

A house was built for Socrates.
His critic friends sought admission.

One thought frankly such plain, bare rooms ought not to please
     A man of his position;
Others faulted the exterior; all agreed
It was too small; there wasn't half the space he'd need;
Greatness must stifle when of such small room possessed.
     "God send true friends enough, I plead,
To fill it," cried Socrates, "and I'll know I'm blessed."
     Friendship lends spaciousness and ease;
Castles are too small to hold the critic's wheeze.
Friend is a title often assumed unfairly
     To disguise insincerities;
     Friends, man's splendor, are found rarely.

21

The Master's Eye

(L'OEIL DU MAÎTRE)

A hunted stag fled for refuge to a stable.
     The oxen lowed, "If you're able,
     Find a safer spot to hide in."
"Too late," he sighed. "Help me, brothers, or I am done.
Please! I can show you a pasture where clear streams run,
My green treasure. Whom but you can I confide in?"
     The oxen were prompt to decide
The stag could use the stable as a place to hide.
He crouched low among them, slowly feeling fitter.
Toward evening the farmhands brought fresh grass and litter.
     As always at that time of day,
     A hundred times they came and went with hay,
     The foreman with them. No one saw a thing.
     The stag's hopes began to take wing.
     In his speech of thanks, he said he would go
As soon as the workmen had left the barnyard clear;
Laboring in the fields, the men would never know

The oxen had sheltered him in his mortal fear.
An ox cleared his throat and rumbled, "Not a bad plan.
But our master has not yet made his inspection.
       Danger lies in that direction.
You have fooled no one unless you can fool that man."
Came the farmer with his men, and glared around.
       "Look!" he barked. "Litter on the ground!
Sweep. Put clean bedding down. More grass on the racks here.
These animals need decent care! Pick up that gear.
You think you can leave the yokes on the floor all year?
Now let me see you make those cobwebs disappear!"
There was little the farmer failed to see and hear.
All at once he stopped short; he has seen a strange head
Bent low among the beasts he was accustomed to.
At last he gave the men work they were glad to do;
       They forked until the stag was dead.
Despite his tears, he made excellent venison,
And feasts aplenty; neighbors flocked to join the fun.
       Phaedrus said—with more elegance—
That for looking at things so that nothing is missed,
       An owner has the surest glance.
I should like to add lovers' glances to the list.

BOOK V

$\underline{3}$
The Very Small Fish and the Fisherman
(LE PETIT POISSON ET LE PÊCHEUR)

Little fish do indeed grow great
If God does grant that they not die,
But if I catch them, I don't wait.
It's imprudent. I fry small fry,
Since I am not sure they'll bite again when bigger.
One dawn a river carp, just a little sprigger,
Took the hook of a hungry fisherman who said,
"Small—but compared to zero, one's a big figure.
There's nothing like fresh fry to give a man vigor."
      Basketed on a leafy bed
The shining infant leapt to show he was not dead
And begged, "Please won't you look again, sir? I won't make
      Half a mouthful. I'm light as air.
      Let me grow large, for pity's sake,
      Then catch me; and o sir, I swear,
Epicures will vie for me. Throw me back, instead
      Of wasting time and toil and care
      Catching a hundred more like me
To make one meal—and poor and bony it would be!"
The man replied, "Though poor and bony as you say,
Fish, you'll find yourself fried for my supper today.
Your speech was a pleasure; I won't call it a waste—
      But fried, you'll really please my taste."

One you've got is worth two that you may be getting;
      Sure things are better than betting.

4

The Hare's Ears

(LES OREILLES DU LIÈVRE)

A lion was gored and found the wound in his pride
      More painful than that in his hide.
      To prevent a repetition
      He decreed the prompt emission
Of all horn-headed creatures from his commonwealth.
Bull, ram, rhinoceros, stag, ox, elephant,
      And every last cerogerant
      At once changed climate for their health.
A hare, noting his ears' shadow rose long and bent,
      Feared some officious visitor
Would think ears horns and call the Court Inquisitor
Who might suspect such ears of satiric intent.
"Goodby, neighbor Cricket. I'm off with the horned gang;
Though these are merely ears, I'm horned enough to hang;
If I had no more ears than an ostrich shows
I'd still expect the worst, and go." The cricket creaked,
      "Horns? You? Poor dumb bunny, the whole world knows
      God made hares' ears so long and peaked."
      "In times like these, logic's foresworn;
They can say I'm triceratops or unicorn
And hang me by that name, found guilty of treason
      With or without horns or reason."

9

The Farmer and His Children

(LE LABOUREUR ET SES ENFANTS)

To those whose wealth is their own work
Funds are always available.
A rich farmer, dying, knowing his sons might shirk
Or quarrel, announced, "Boys, this farm is salable . . .
But don't sell! or you'll lose the rich inheritance
     My parents buried on this farm
     During a national alarm.
That gold is here somewhere, and you have every chance
—If you combine your strength—to find it and be rich.
Once the fields are harvested, dig from ditch to ditch.
Plow deep. Rake. Sieve. You can find what they could bury!
     Dig it twice, if necessary."
He died; his sons dug; his lie kept the land from harm,
So that by fall the deep-plowed fields had felt the charm;
     Crops doubled in exuberance.
They found no gold, but their father's vigilance
     Had taught them how to measure
     Good work as a man's real treasure.

10

The Mountain in Labor

(LA MONTAGNE QUI ACCOUCHE)

A mountain was in labor and
Groaned with loud tremendous groans.
The locals rushed to be on hand
To see what great thing stretched its bones—
Moons? Stars? Or a new Paris, God's guest-house?
     Well, the mountain brought forth a mouse.

When I think of this fable
Which, though silly, makes good sense.
I recall writers, able
To brag in the future tense:
"What a book I'm about to write!
Zeus, thunder, war—what drama! some plot! dynamite!"
They trumpet promises, but what's their work of art?
A fart.

12
The Doctors
(LES MÉDECINS)

Doctors All-Is-Lost and All-Is-Well were both called
To see a sick man. Dr. All-Is-Well was sure
The patient would soon be well. His colleague, appalled,
Said, "Doctor, I differ. There's no hope of a cure."
While they argued what to do for which prognosis
Dr. All-Is-Lost's views reached apotheosis:
The man died. Now hear how each doctor, unshaken,
Claimed the death proved him right. "I told you so," one said;
The other shook his head. "He died having taken
Your advice, poor man. He should have tried mine instead."

13
The Hen that Laid Golden Eggs
(LA POULE AUX OEUFS D'OR)

Greed-gripped men can keep nothing long, for all their greed.
Once a hen, fabulous indeed,
Laid a punctual daily egg of solid gold.
Her owner, being avaricious,

Was in haste, and split her. This was injudicious;
Her innards were ordinary, useless, and soon cold;
Her deeds had been her wealth, for him alone deployed.
He learned too late it was his own good he'd destroyed.
       You mean men, read this tale aright.
We've seen so many lately—one big sorry crew,
When their greedy, lazy, get-rich-quick schemes fall through
And they're poor, not rich, overnight.

15

The Stag and the Vine
(LE CERF ET LA VIGNE)

Thanks to some vines—the tall kind that grow densely twined
Between woodland and farmland—a stag in full flight
From the hunt took refuge out of the hunter's sight.
The master called off the dogs, fooled by the green blind.
The hunt rode on. The stag soon dismissed his last doubt
And cropped the vine leaves with ungrateful arrogance.
Back rode the hunt; one glimpse, and they harried him out.
       Dying, he sighed, "It is not chance
But justice that is meting out my punishment.
Learn of me, hard of heart!" But the pack was intent
On the division of the spoils; greed without grief
Hastened his death. Such is the final abjection
Due him who turns against what was once his relief,
       Comfort, and protection.

16

The Snake and the File
(LE SERPENT ET LA LIME)

A snake visited a nearby watchmaker's place
(Even the Swiss find snakes inauspicious neighbors).
In, out, up, down, he looked for worms and found no trace;
        Angry after fruitless labors
He chose a steel file and gnawed at a steady pace
Till the courteous file remarked without rancor
    "Enough: I'm as inedible as an anchor;
        Don't die chewing on me—a thing
        You wouldn't want if you could get!
        Use every weapon, jaws, coils, sting;
        I shall remain here, unscratched yet;
        Though you wear out sting, coils, jaws
        I submit only to time's laws."

Critics, this time it's to you I refer.
You attack fine, true-tempered art as if it were
        Your own diet of worm and frond
But nothing you do can scarify in men's eyes
        The splendid things you criticize;
They thwart your rage: as lead, as steel, as diamond.

20

The Bear and the Two Friends
(L'OURS ET LES DEUX COMPAGNONS)

        Two friends, short of cash, went to see
        A furrier to sell the hide
        Of a bear not yet caught, to be
Killed by them on order—or so they certified.

The fur of this king among bears would guarantee,
In winter's worst freeze, comfort worth its weight in gold;
It was big enough to line not one coat, but three,
And so increase the furrier's profit threefold.
As Dindon praised his sheep (described by Rabelais),
So they praised the bear that was not yet theirs in fact.
Promising prompt delivery, they got their pay.
They made for the woods, and soon had the great bear tracked—
Or it tracked them, perhaps; it loomed, and charged the pair.
Fear stunned them. Business is business—but death is death;
Faced with the bear's rage, they no longer wasted breath
Considering profits; they considered the bear.
One scrambled up a tree, and found himself alone;
        His friend had fallen like a stone.
Motionless and unbreathing he lay playing dead,
        Hoping for safety in deceit;
        For bears, as he had heard it said,
Walk away from motionless, breathless, lifeless meat.
The fool bear must have heard the same thing. Grandiose,
He bent to the body and cautiously pawed it;
        To avoid being defrauded
He turned it over and brought his giant muzzle close
        To the man's nostrils, then said,
"A corpse! I'm off; it's already begun to stink."
He vanished into the forest, shaking his head.
The tree-climber watched him go, then quick as a wink
Clambered down and ran to congratulate his friend
On his narrow escape from a fate worse than dread,
Worse than their mutual loss of the hide. He said,
        "I watched him turn you, and bend;
        I saw how close your two heads got—
        What did he whisper to you there?"
        "He advised me, 'No matter what,
Don't sell the bearskin till you've caught and killed your bear.'"

21

The Donkey Dressed in the Lion-Skin

(L'ANE VÊTU DE LA PEAU DU LION)

A donkey disguised in a lifelike lion-skin
    Filled the animal folk with dread.
    Though without bravery within,
    He looked so fierce the others fled
Until, worse luck for him, one long ear tip stuck out
    And proved him donkey beyond doubt.
    His owner chased him, stick in hand.
When passers-by saw that, they could not understand,
    For few men's courage runs so quick
    They can hunt lions with a stick.

    All fair France, now and heretofore,
Has sung the praises of many a miscreant
    The sum of whose accomplishment
    Was a false front, and nothing more.

BOOK VI

7
The Mule Boasts of His Genealogy
(LE MULET SE VANTANT DE SA GÉNÉALOGIE)

The bishop's proud mule boasted of nobility,
    Of what did his mother the mare,
    Of her gifts, to which he was heir;
    He bragged with long facility.
For his mother, the mare, had done this and gone there,
    And he felt, if schoolbooks were fair,
    Her life would edify a class.
Those days, he scorned hauling doctors or priests around;
Old, he was shipped to a mill where grain was ground.
It was then he remembered his father, the ass.

    Though misfortune may do no more
    Than teach a fool what minds are for,
    Just that one lesson adduces
    How misfortune has its uses.

8
The Old Man and the Donkey
(LE VIEILLARD ET L'ANE)

Near his country's border an old man riding past
    Saw a flowered field, greenly grassed.

He dismounted to let his tired donkey run
  Over the meadow in the sun.
  It kicked up its heels, capered, brayed,
  Then cropped the grass till it had made
  Patches like lawns, neatly cleared.
  An enemy soldier appeared.
  "Fly!" cried the old man. "We must flee!"
  The donkey answered, "Why? Why me?
Would your enemies make me carry double freight?"
"No," the man yelled, fleeing. The donkey shrugged. "I'll wait;
Run, since men kill men. But who cares who's my master?
  No enemy army irks me;
  I just hate the man who works me.
  Frankly, war is *your* disaster."

9
_____

The Stag Who Saw His Reflection

(LE CERF SE VOYANT DANS L'EAU)

  A stag at a crystalline brook
  Admired his antlers' broad spread.
  He was delighted with his head
  But he could hardly bear to look
  At his thin legs. "Stick stick stick stick,
Each stick with a wee tiny hoof . . . they make me sick!
They're all out of proportion compared to the rest."
Lifting a hoof to see, he sighed as he said it.
"My antlers crown the crowns of bushes; they're the best.
  But these feet do me no credit."
    The moment he had spoken,
    Bloodhounds bayed and made him scud
    For the woods through flying mud.
    His antlers, still unbroken
  But breakable, kept getting caught,

Stopping him. To stop was to court
The death he sped from on swift feet.
He lived because he was so fleet.
After, he recanted and had the wit to scorn
His merely decorative horn.

We prize the beautiful; the useful we disdain.
Which we need, we may learn sadly.
That stag had agile feet yet they made him complain
While he suffered antlers gladly.

10

The Hare and the Tortoise
(LE LIÈVRE ET LA TORTUE)

Despite what you do, lost time disappears for good,
As the hare in this next fable learned to his cost.
"Will you race me? Tortoise asked him. "I wish you would."
"Me race you!" Hare laughed. "Why run? you've already lost.
Who's your medical adviser?
You may need a tranquilizer."
"In spite of what you think of it,"
She said, "I don't intend to quit,
At least until we've raced."
They agreed; their bets were soon placed,
(What they bet, who refereed there,
I scarcely think I need repeat.)
Now this was no cage bunny, but a wild field hare
Alive because no dog could match his swift, strong feet;
He could have won at once. But he stretched on the grass
Breathing deep, watching cloud-shapes pass,
Musing, "Poor Tortoise. She plods. I'm invincible.
She's like an old school principal,
Pompously plugging on, dragging her feet."

She did plug patiently ahead
While Hare dreamed of how to compete
Without seeming to bother his head.
"Casual victories look more victorious,"
    He thought, and planned to be glorious.
    Tortoise hurried slowly ahead
Pacing herself to the race as a whole,
    Steadily pressing for the goal.
Hare looked, then stared after her, astounded;
She was almost in reach of the goal they had set.
He sprang into action; he leaped and he bounded
In vain. Tortoise had won both the race and their bet.
She cried, "See, Hare, I won; I'm here first, and not you!"
    She added with a little sniff,
    "What would have happened, friend Hare, if
You'd had your house to carry, too?"

12

The Sun and the Frogs

(LE SOLEIL ET LES GRENOUILLES)

When the king was married, wine banished all care
    Throughout a jubilant nation.
Aesop alone looked on their glad celebration
    And beheld stupidity bare.
He said, "When the sun once proposed to contemplate
    The selection of a wife
Frogdom's croak of protest rose to the ears of Fate:
    "Help! Must we be ruled out of life?
    Kind Fate, protect us in our bogs!
If he has sons, what will become of frogs?
One sun is as great a glory as we can stand.
    With six or so more like him in command,
We are done for; our whole world will go up in fog.

If suns put an end to marsh, pond, and pleasant stream,
    We'll croak beside the Styx' black gleam."
  As philosophers, frogs are reckoned mute,
But these had a sense of logic I call astute.

13

The Farmer and the Snake
(LE VILLAGEOIS ET LE SERPENT)

    A farmer in an Aesop tale,
    Who matched great kindness with small brain,
    Patrolled his farm, up hill, down dale,
    Through bitter winter snow and rain.
He came on a snake half-covered with snow, quite still,
Half frozen, half dead, stretched stiff on the icy hill.
    He picked it up, for pity's sake,
And hurried worrying home with the dying snake,
Imprudently forgetting the cost of kind acts.
    It lay on his hearth stiff as wire.
    He brought in more logs and the ax,
    Chopped wood and blew to build the fire,
And smiled when it stirred. But as soon as it could rise
Though feeble still, it reared up in wrath from the floor.
Hissing, the snake fixed the farmer with cold surprise,
Coiled, poised its head, and tried to strike between the eyes.
Its whole intent was to kill its benefactor.
"Filth!" the farmer muttered. "What did I save you for?"
Red with righteous wrath, he grabbed the ax as he spoke,
And at once, where one snake had writhed, two writhed instead.
    Three snake shapes formed at his next stroke:
    A tail, a body, and a head
That tried as he swept them outside to reunite.
    The door shut, he said, "Good snake, good night!"

All ungrateful creatures, you see,
Die in well-deserved misery.
Kindness is good but ought not to be
Compounded with stupidity.

15

The Bird-Catcher, the Hawk, and the Lark

(L'OISELEUR, L'AUTOUR, ET L'ALOUETTE)

We use our neighbor's sin to draw
Attention from our own misdeeds
Despite the universal law,
"Spare others if you would be spared," which wise men heed.
Mirrors lured birds to where a boy's wide net hung looped.
Down came a lark, attracted by a phantom flash.
At the same instant a hovering hawk stooped,
     His lethal claws ready to slash.
The small songbird caught sight, just in time, of the net
And veered up singing, right into the hawk's steel clutch.
The hawk cut short the soaring song, without regret,
     Indeed with joy—perhaps too much;
He was so absorbed in unfeathering his prey
He struck the net. It held; he could not break away.
He tried to plead. "Boy, have I ever done you wrong?
     Spare me, bird-catcher! let me go."
The boy replied, "That little lark if he still had his song
     Could say the same to you, you know."

16
The Horse and the Donkey
(LE CHEVAL ET L'ANE)

One creature helps another, turn and turn about.
    If your colleague's time should run out,
      His cares drop from him—and are yours.
A donkey trudged beside a strong, proud horse whose back
Bore nothing of more consequence than his own tack.
The greatly burdened donkey gasped—he had good cause—
And begged for a little help from his big neighbor.
"Otherwise," he brayed, "I shall die here on the road.
Do grant this last request. To your strength, half my load
Would be child's play." The horse piaffed. "No! Slave, your labor
Suits you well; you were born to it." He turned his head.
When he looked again, the exhausted beast was dead.
      He saw no error in his pride
      Until the men loaded him down
      To haul the donkey's pack to town
      And added the poor donkey's hide.

17
The Dog that Dropped His Prey for Its Shadow
(LE CHIEN QUI LÂCHE SA PROIE POUR L'OMBRE)

    Men practice self-deception.
    Numberless samples of the race
    With endless misconception
    Claim shadows are real, and give chase.

Aesop's "Dog at the River" might speed their cure:
The stream mirrored his prey. It escaped while, allured
By the image, he plunged in to make it secure—

But it too fled. He fought, almost drowned, swam, endured,
And staggered ashore having lost these three:
A hope, a truth, a fantasy.

19

The Charlatan
(LE CHARLATAN)

The world's supply of charlatans never runs short.
Crowd-dazzlers spring afresh, unsought
In every age, and every state.
Some are heroic in circuses, fairs, or plays;
Or boast of how they can orate
More movingly than Cicero.
One such loved his own eloquence
So much he claimed without pretense
That his inspired skill could teach
Farmboys and fools pure golden speech.
"Better yet, fetch a donkey, a poor dumb creature,"
He cried. "Using only my matchless rhetoric
I'll make a genius of him, quick—
In fact, I'll make him a preacher!"
The prince heard, and called the braggart rhetorician.
He announced, "My stables confine
An ass who's really asinine.
Put him in preaching condition."
"My law is your command," replied our charlatan.
"Take this gold," said the prince, "and plan
For his first speech ten years from now,
Should you not keep your boastful vow
I shall invoke the law and come to applaud
While they properly strangle you in the town square,
As you wear signboards saying, 'Fraud,'
Plus two long ass-ears in your hair."

Eyeing the gold and donkey, the braggart agreed.
He heard, for cold comfort, a precious courtier say,
"Lucky you—though you die, that last speech will succeed!
The prince and all his court will come to see the deed—
You'll have a greater audience than any play.
Use pathos, and you'll die ruling the hearts of men;
      Condemned thieves will quote you with tears!"
      The fraud winked. "Friend, have no fears.
      The prince, the ass, or I, by then
      Will have been dead and gone for years."

      He was right. No prudent man can
      Bank on living a ten-year span.
      Relish life while you have the breath.
In ten years, one of three who read, will have met death.

EPILOGUE

      It's time I put a stop to this.
      I dread tomes. I take from a theme
      Flowers, not soil analysis;
      Fit words and few best suit my scheme.
      Now for a time I shall be still
      To gather strength and shape my skill
      For the task Love sets me to do:
      Ruled by Love, my lifelong guide,
      I shall change old themes for new.
      Love's least wish must be gratified.
So I shall paint Love's pride, Psyche; Damon, you ask
That I show her smiles and tears; I accept the task.
      Perhaps my work will earn the thrill
      That thoughts of her can sometimes be;
Perhaps—what luck—the Love-god, for my efforts, will
      Henceforward grant me amnesty.

"Education" (Book VIII, 24)

Third and Fourth Parts

BOOK VII

3

The Rat that Retired from Worldly Affairs
(LE RAT QUI S'EST RETIRÉ DU MONDE)

Here's a legend told in the Levant:
Rat had tired of strife; the age was hysterical,
      Its mobs fought for cash and loud cant.
      His ideal was calm, spherical,
      Spiritual, but there to touch;
      He chose a cheese, the kind called Dutch,
And vowed, "I'm a hermit. Race of Rats, I recede
      To gnaw forth all I'll ever need:
Both regular meals and hermetic asylum
Befitting my rank in the rodent phylum."
Heaven blesses hermits, they say. After that vow,
      Rat grew plump. Gladness oiled his brow.
      A poor Ratdom delegation
      Approached our lone hermit's station
Having fled, hands empty, to tell Ratdom's allies
      Catdom had struck them by surprise.
Knowing their allies, if warned, would save their nation
      They begged Rat lend the wherewithal
Since diplomats, though desperate, can't live on air,
      And Ratdom's treasury was so bare
      It had nothing to spare at all—

Temporarily, of course. Once their allies learned,
     Fortune's tides would be swiftly turned.
     "O my poor friends!" the hermit groaned.
"I own nothing. Holy poverty sets me free,
     Above mundane cares. Don't you see,
     This wealth is heaven's; to me, it's loaned;
On trust, you might say, not mine to share. But I'll pray
That heaven trust you and lend you some too, someday."
     He humbly smiled and, what's more,
     First forgave them, then shut the door.
     Whom do I mean, do you suppose,
     By this self-souled rat ascetic?
     Not our clergy, goodness knows,
But some idolatrous lot, old, bad, emetic.

4 and 5

The Heron; The Young Woman

(LE HÉRON; LA FILLE)

A long-legged heron, enjoying a private walk,
His long-beaked head nodding above his long neck-stalk,
     Strolled down the riverbank one day.
Thanks to fine weather the water was clear as air;
A carp and a shining pike moved fluently there,
     Turn and return, in easy play.
The heron could have dined then, had it been his wish;
They swam so close he had but to stoop and catch them.
     Appetite half bid him snatch them,
     But his diet told him to fish
Only when really hungry, no nibbling allowed.
That time came, and he scanned the stream only to find
     What swam there was not to his mind.
He saw tench, those small mud-fed carp, but was too proud
(Like Horace's too-fastidious city rat)

To dine on plain common fare. "Scat!"
He murmured. "I think it correct
For some to eat tench. Not herons—herons expect
Meals with no smudge of mud or odor of smudge on."
The next fish he noticed were some little gudgeon.
"Ridiculous stream!" he exclaimed in high dudgeon,
"It takes more than that to open a heron's beak!"
It took less. Shortly the hungry epicene
  Mourned that no fish were to be seen.
At last he gladly gobbled down, without critique,
  A snail, a small one, very lean.
  Let us all be less difficult.
Be easy to please, if you would often exult.
Total loss, or the risk of it, is greed's great bane.
  Avoid self-defeating disdain;
Learn to make do with a genteel sufficiency.
Not only herons fail to learn this lesson well;
Listen, my fellow men, for it occurs to me
That our ways provide another tale I can tell:
  A beauty who was rather proud
  Planned what kind of man she'd espouse
He'd be young, well built, handsome, much above the crowd;
Not frigid nor jealous nor yet content to drowse.
  Further, to earn her marriage vows,
  He would be rich and nobly bred,
Intelligent too—a paragon would do her.
A kindly Fate sent paragons to view her
  And even to ask her to wed.
The beauty found them all too trivial by half.
"What, I? What, them? You can't be serious," she said.
"I'm not meant for creatures that merely make me laugh."
  One she found indelicate, crude;
Another had a nose whose very shape was rude.
Her discovery of each new mortal defect
  That no other eye could detect
  She did not lay to pride, but traced

To her rare and exquisite taste.
When she'd scorned the fine offers, middling suitors came
To offer life, wealth, heart, and name.
She mocked, "By what right would that fool open his door
And there find . . . me? Do I then seem so desperate
He thinks he is all I'm meant for?
To be alone poses no threat
To me; and I sleep well at night."
So she stuffed herself with self-congratulation.
Age spoiled her looks; farewell love and adulation;
One empty year passed, then two, worsening her plight.
Regret set in; older with each new day, she felt
This charm, that smile, those tricks, even love pale and melt
Till her features shocked and displeased.
Then came the paints, dyes, and creams, hundreds, but none eased
Her losing fight with time, the impalpable thief.
Skilled repair can bring full relief
To ruined towns—a pity we're not competent
To reverse the disfigurement
Of a time-ruined face. She grew less insolent;
Her mirror admonished, "Find a husband soon, do!"
I don't know what other desire urged her too:
Desire can have its way, even with the proud.
Choosy no more, she chose, and no one gainsaid her
As she triumphantly found and promptly allowed
Some poor old lumpkin to wed her.

7

The Lion Holds Court
(LA COUR DU LION)

Great King Lion once thought it was time that he saw
Samples of the beasts he ruled by natural law.
Far and near went criers, crying,

Accompanied by deputies,
Leaving parchments bravely flying
From all town squares and highway trees.
All beasts by this proclamation
Had a royal invitation
For month-long court festivities
Starring a comical baboon.
This last touch showed what a tycoon
The king was, and what wealth he had.
So to his Louvre came the beasts as they were bade.
Lovely Louvre! pardon his palace,
That slaughterhouse, stinking of dark bloody malice.
Bear, a hapless vegetarian, held his nose—
A fatal error; Lion, roaring fury, rose
And smote him; Bear next sniffed the atmosphere in hell.
Monkey tried praise: he praised it all, the place, the smell,
The murder, too. "True majesty does all things well—
Even your air is rich! like ambergris, perhaps?
Garlic buds? lilies!" "You lie! Though fools are courted
With lies, I'm not!" Lion snorted,
Sideswiping Monkey who fell in mortal collapse.
The king's will, like Caligula's, was full of traps.
At truth and lies he took offense;
Both served to keep his rage intense.
Noticing Fox, he roared, "You there! What do you smell?
Don't stand on ceremony. Tell me exactly."
Friend Fox bowed matter-of-factly.
"Sire, with my sinus trouble, I simply can't tell,
Can't smell a thing." It served to quell
The royal wrath, and teach us too
That courtiers who hope to be well received should be
Sparing, not lavish, in praise and in honesty—
And learn to speak as Normans or Vermonters do.

9

The Coach and the Fly
(LE COCHE ET LA MOUCHE)

Up a steep, ill-built, sandy road came foamed with sweat
Six draft horses dragging the noon coach. Though broad-set
     They made hard progress up the hill.
The passengers—women, priests, old men—descended;
The horses struggled, their morning freshness ended.
A busy fly approached them, buzzing with good will.
Thinking her noise would help and stings help even more,
She stung as if that were what they were waiting for.
     Feeling she was gaining control,
She checked the shafts, sat on the coachman's nose, and bit;
     Seeing the coach grudging roll
     And men walk, she grew sure of it.
Her self-image radiant, Dame Fly seemed to be
Like a field general in battle; confident,
Hurrying everywhere at once, she came and went
Cheering her subordinates on to victory.
     As leaders will do, she complained
All the work was left to her; hers each inch they gained;
The horses were hers alone to help and harry—
     The monk read his breviary,
Slow as mud, too! some woman was singing—singing,
At a time like that! Nobly Dame Fly went winging
Back and forth, giving the troops a piece of her mind,
     Spurring on those who hung behind.
The horses strained and strove; the coach attained the crest.
Proudly Dame Fly told the horses, "Before you rest
Pay me for my pains as I know you long to do,
Since thanks to me I have brought you all safely through."

It is also thus with those busy nosey-faced
     Men who poke at others' affairs

Think nothing right but what is theirs;
They dart in everywhere, just begging to be chased.

10

The Milkmaid and the Pot of Milk
(LA LAITIÈRE ET LE POT AU LAIT)

Milkmaid Perrette set out for the market one day.
    Her crock, held the old-fashioned way,
Was poised on a proper cushion upon her head.
Perrette was a lissome young wife, and strong though slight;
A farm girl with tucked-up skirts and flat shoes, she sped
    Poised as birds are, easy and light.
    On she strode, figuring the gains
    The milk would bring her for her pains.
The full profit, she reckoned, would certainly buy
A hundred good nest eggs; with much warmth and good drains
She would help them all hatch, and not a chick would die.
    "Chicks can be raised at home," thought she;
"I'd scare the foxes off some clever way, then buy
    A lovely piglet almost free
By selling extra chicks and eggs. I'd need a sty,
And fatten my pig cheap on table-scraps and rye;
In no time he'd be worth triple the price I paid.
I could sell him quite dear and put the profits by
And then, why not, I'd have a bigger stable made
To house a calf and cow, and make the farm complete!"
The vision of the future was so clear, so sweet,
She jumped for joy. She jumped; the milk-crock jumped, and fell,
And smashed. Gone cow, calf, pigs, chicks, dreams, all smashed as well!
Leaving her puddled wealth, poor Perrette in tears
    And carrying only an excuse
    Went home to her husband with fears
    Of deserving his worst abuse.

Her tale claims a certain glory
In a farce, "The Milk-Pot Story."

All men dream joys few men attain.
I dream of my castle in Spain,
Like Perrette, like heroes fictional and real,
    Like fools, like friends, like you, I feel
The sweetness of waking dreams and their soft appeal.
Their truthless flattery lifts up the humdrum soul:
    All wealth is mine; fair women kneel;
    My honors make an aureole;
I bravely challenge a scoundrel and knock him dead;
I march on a foreign tyrant and take his head.
    Oh, I'm wise, I'm well-loved, I'm king.
I'm bright and kind and brave and free
Until some trifle calls me, and I reinstate
    The plain self I was born to be.

13

The Two Roosters

(LES DEUX COQS)

Two roosters lived in peace. A hen entered the scene,
    And battle flames filled them with fire.
You, Love, lost Troy; you struck and left women to keen
    When the venom of war's desire
Sped in the blood of gods and men, and with it spilled.
The cocks fought on, eager to see each other killed.
Summoned by battle shrieks and squawks, the neighborhood
Came in a crested crowd to watch. The winner won
    Helen—and Helens. All he could
Wish for was his. The loser left the barnyard sun
And hid himself to mourn loves lost and glories gone—
    Loves whose joys his brash rival snatched
Before his very eyes. He skulked there in the barn
Eyeing the winner, wishing he'd never been hatched.

His courage grew fat with hate; he tried exercise,
Beating wings on flanks, on air, and against the wind;
    He sharpened his beak to pierce and prize;
    He made his rage war-disciplined—
To no use. His foe flew above their residence
  And crowed his heroic battle story.
    A vulture in his audience
    Heard him—farewell love and glory!
An endless pride perished in the swift vulture's grip.
    The cycle spun without a slip
    And Helen Hen wheeled into view.
    Taking up her same old station
    Amid hennish agitation—
    For Helen had her rivals, too.
Fortune's pleasure lies in such tricks and surprises.
By their own harsh pride, harsh proud victors are undone.
Beware: the moment of greatest danger rises
    After the battle has been won.

16

The Cat, the Weasel, and the Small Rabbit

(LE CHAT, LA BELETTE, ET LE PETIT LAPIN)

    A rabbit had a house, until
    Weasel slipped across the sill.
    She brought her things at once, of course,
And began to redecorate without remorse.
The owner was out; such was his morning habit.
He had gone like a poetical young rabbit
    To the dew-wet wild thyme and gorse
To pay ecstatic homage to the risen sun.
He leaped, nibbled, and left with his day well begun.
Weasel was waiting for him at the window frame.
He cried, "Gods of hearth and home, what's this!" as he came.
Deprived of his ancestral home, he shouted, loud,

"Leave, Miss Weasel! or I'll chase
All the rats that come near this place!"
"Leave yourself! I stay. Two in this case is a crowd,"
Snapped she. "Haven't you ever heard of rights? I'm right.
The earth is his who sits in it.
Not that this hole is worth a fight—
It is much too small; I have to lie flat to fit—
But suppose it were a palace,
Which it's not. Can you prove title? Can law define
Descendance in the rabbit line?
Where's your deed? It may belong to Al or Alice
Or anyone. It may be mine!"
Rabbit said, "I can prove it's mine and prove it pat.
By the basic laws of custom and use, to me
Comes my paternal inheritance, clear and free—
Which makes you an illegal occupant, you see.
From Charles to James to me, John, came this habitat."
Weasel shrieked, "Enough of that!
Let's ask judicial Felix to help us agree."
Cat Felix was famous both for his pious looks
And for the law he owned in books.
He was sleek and round, and slippery as a wet stone;
And tackled every subject known.
Rabbit agreed to arbitrate
With Felix as judge advocate.
He heard half their explanation
And said, "Will you please step up closer, then restate?
Right up close; I'm so deaf. From old age, I suppose."
They obeyed and advanced to just under his nose.
Felix judged the distance, smiled, and shot out both paws.
He resolved their quarrel for good
By impounding them both in his terrible claws
And judiciously eating them as a cat should.
I find those flies foolish who, in want of a rest,
Think spiderwebs look soft and put them to the test.

17

The Head and the Tail of the Snake
(LA TÊTE ET LA QUEUE DU SERPENT)

Neither of the snake's two ends
Is numbered with mankind's friends.
Both are tools of Fate, whether
Used singly or together.
Death-sting Tail and death-bite Head
Argued, as leader and led,
A question they found immense:
     Precedence.
Head's right was supported by a long tradition.
    Tail asked the gods why she went
       Subsequent.
    "Must this be my position,
    Slavishly obedient?
I go where Head drags me; this form of government
    Makes me serve without a voice;
    Born equal if different,
    She has, and I lack, free choice.
    We are of one blood—your gift!—
    Why then am I her sequel?
    Surely our works are equal;
    Both stings are deadly and swift.
    One fair turn is all I ask,
    O Gods, in justice not greed.
    Let Head follow while I lead;
    I promise to take my task
    With such serious restraint
    That Head will have no complaint."
The gods with cruel kindness heard Tail and agreed.
When gods are generous, let suppliants beware.
A blind fool's dreams, come true, may prove a blind fool's snare.

So in this case. Tail could no more see where to lead
     Out amid the blaze of noon,
     Than if wound in a cocoon.
     She ran them into stones, trees,
     Men, and other enemies.
Down the black Styx* went Tail, hauling Head in her wake.
Unhappy the nations that make the same mistake.

The mythological river that encircles Hell seven times.

BOOK VIII

5

The Man and the Flea
(L'HOMME ET LA PUCE)

We make the gods tired with frantic prayers and pleas
For help in things beneath even man's attention.
We would have the Olympians in constant apprehension
Inspecting us all, counting how often gnats sneeze.
We assume that every move living creatures make
Means as much to the gods as if lives were at stake
And shakes Olympus with the same fascination
The gods knew when Greece stood against Priam's nation.*
Once a fool felt his shoulder bitten by a flea;
It escaped him and bided its time in his sheet.
"Hercules!" he prayed. "Here's a hydra to defeat—
Purge the earth of it next spring—and remember me!
Do something, Jupiter; I'm annoyed, can't you see?"
In this the poor man saw nothing ridiculous;
He thought the gods must, should he be pediculous,
Let loose the lightning and cast their thunderbolts free.

The Trojan war, which inspired Homer's Iliad *and* Odyssey.

12

The Pig, the Goat, and the Sheep

(LE COCHON, LA CHÈVRE, ET LE MOUTON)

A farmer put a sheep, a plump pig, and a goat
Into his cart, and off to the fair they went.
The creatures were, though unaware, all in one boat,
Soon to be sold for slaughter in the market tent.
  These passengers would see no clowns
  Or comic dancers in gold gowns.
  Sir Swine, despite the farmer's frowns,
Squealed as if he already glimpsed the butchers' knives,
Squealed without ceasing, deafening the patient pair
That rode beside him. They had led more sheltered lives
And had no inkling why he shrilled in such despair;
  They could not see anything wrong.
"Pig!" the farmer called. "Next time you won't come along
If you don't stop that! Your friends are ashamed of you.
They are enjoying the change, the fresh air, the view—
See how they behave. Don't be a vulgarian!
Take a hint from friend sheep there. He's wise. He keeps cool."
  Said Sir Swine, "He's a fool!
If he guessed where you're steering this caravan,
How he'd howl! These two innocents aren't frightened
  But if you tell them what's in store
  They'll bleat then, and shriek and implore.
They think they're going to the fair to be lightened,
The goat of her milk, the sheep of wool—that may be.
  But we know about fairs, we swine.
  I know what destiny is mine—
  Pork! That will be the death of me.
  Farewell, fair world!" He did define
What was coming, being smart and energetic;
But when we dread what we are sure we still must face
To express either fear or grief is out of place;
Those best behaved are often those least prophetic.

17

The Donkey and the Dog

(L'ANE ET LE CHIEN)

Nature's law makes us depend on mutual aid.
      Though most donkeys are decent beasts,
      One time a donkey felt released
      From the golden rule he'd obeyed.
He and a dog, sober tourists, went here and there
      A dignified, hard-working pair,
      With their owner, who thought he led.
The man napped. The donkey found the grass good, and said,
      "First-class pasture!" He kept grazing.
      "Thistleless but great—it's amazing!"
Thistles can't be on every bill of fare;
It would be too much to expect at every meal.
      Indeed, experts at feasting feel
      True feasts are feasts because they're rare.
      Well, the donkey was satisfied.
Famished, the dog barked quite politely at his side,
"It's sad to dine alone. I'll join you—if you'll bend;
My food's in your saddlebag, easily untied."
No answer. The donkey refused his hungry friend
      For fear he'd lose a moment's cropping.
      He cropped and cropped, no sign of stopping,
      Till much later he suggested,
"It's not my place to grant what you have requested.
Patience! Ask your master—when he's rested.
Mustn't be selfish; let him sleep unmolested.
      He'll wake up soon enough, you know.
      Relax; the wait will do you good."
      A wolf raced toward them from the wood,
Starving hungry. The donkey brayed, "Help, help! Haroo!"
The dog smiled. "Patience. You can ask for proper advice
From your master when he wakes. That's the thing to do.
In the meantime I'd start running if I were you.

Fast. Don't stop. And don't be selfish. It isn't nice.
If the wolf outruns you, relax, and break his jaw.
You're new-shod; take my word, that's what iron's for.
Kick; it will do you good." But the wolf, more concise,
Killed the donkey. I conclude that on any score,
      "Help each other" is natural law.

19

The Value of Learning
(L'AVANTAGE DE LA SCIENCE)

Two city friends had a dispute
On how to live and why men act.
One, though poor, was schooled and resolute.
One was rich and dull; since he lacked
Both sense and learning, he attacked.
"I'm better than you. You know it.
Goods are what's good—all lives show it—
And I own far more goods than you."
There spoke a stupid man. What can mere objects do
To earn their owner true respect?
Such reasons reason must reject.
Yet the man urged his friend, "Retract!"
      Face the fact—
Though you think your ideas matter—
At your table, who gets fatter?
Your nose stuck in a book, your writing finger blacked,
You freeze in your one thin suit, so you're rheumatic.
Innkeepers hide guests like you up in the attic.
You pay no servant but yourself. We could subtract
      You from the economy fast—
      Just take away nothing; that's you.
      Without men like me, states can't last.
I spend. I employ men. And girls! And when I'm through
The economic growth is something to behold.

Men who make or sell or serve depend on my gold . . .
And you do, too, for all your brains; you dedicate
      Your high-priced books to financiers,
      Begging alms. Now, who's second-rate?"
      The mockery fell on deaf ears.
      The wise man said nothing at all,
Having too much to say; why wound the incurable?
He sought no revenge. It came, full and durable,
But not from him. War raged; they saw their city fall.
      The enemy took it; they fled.
      No man helped the dull fool; instead
      He was laughed off with bitter mirth.
All men welcomed the wise man with joy. The last word
      Was his who had remained unheard.
Lack them or like them, art and learning have real worth.

23

The Torrent and the River
(LE TORRENT ET LA RIVIÈRE)

      Down the mountain a torrent streamed
      So swift, so bright and boisterous,
Neither man nor beast dared ford it; to most it seemed
      A synonym for dangerous.
      Travelers went the long way round,
      Fearing its force and vortices.
A lone rider, hard pressed by thieves, plunged in—and found
He and his horse crossed it with ease,
Despite its turmoil, speed, and bad reputation.
      His fears fled. With great elation—
      Though the thieves were still in pursuit—
He raced on, till another river blocked his way.
      This one flowed sleepy, calm, and mute,
      Reflecting the soft summer day
Tranquilly between smooth banks of crystalline sand.

Never doubting he would soon reach the further strand,
Into the water he rode, boldly, without pause.
      He was safe enough from outlaws
For it was to a stronger, hidden foe he lost.
      He and his mount never crossed;
      Drawn darkly down by the unknown deep
They rode into the shadow world of final sleep.
      The silent man is dangerous;
      His calm cloaks secrets he must keep.
      The loud are just impetuous.

24

Education
(L'ÉDUCATION)

Caesar and Sloppot were dogs of one litter, born
To a line of brave, smart, biddable thoroughbreds.
Different masters gave them training, work, and beds.
One was schooled to hunt; one chased kitchen mice with scorn;
Both lost their registered names. Education
      Strengthened every good attribute
In Caesar's blood, and made his brother a sly brute,
Much kicked, so ill-fed he earned the appellation
      "Sloppot," by association.
Caesar, trained for high adventure, gained in repute.
He led the hunt, brought down deer and boar, and became
One dog called Caesar who really deserved the name.
He was bred with care, so that no unworthy bride
Ever mixed lesser gifts with his prized chromosomes.
Sloppot was let run, and gave his brief affection
      To brides from underprivileged homes;
      These efforts produced, I admit,
The kitchen dogs that now turn every Frenchman's spit—
A soft lot, averse to danger, the spit-dogs are
      Miles beneath hunters like Caesar.

Not all adults show likeness to their families,
But all show care and schooling—or the lack of these.
How many valiant Caesars sleep unsuspected
In Sloppots whose education is neglected!

BOOK IX

3

The Monkey and the Leopard
(LE SINGE ET LE LÉOPARD)

Monkey and Leopard went to seek
Glory and fortune at the Fair.
Each had a booth—and a technique.
Leopard roared his pitch. "Come one, come all, come see! Where
But here is there a hide the king himself calls rare?
A hide that same king hopes to wear
When I'm through with it! For it's speckled so neatly
And it's marbled so discreetly,
Spotted and mottled, completely!"
He drew a motley crowd that bought its way inside
Then left. It doesn't take long to look at a hide.
Mate Monkey was there waiting. He called, "Come all ye!
Tricks and capers! Magic, laughter! See the monkey!
You want diversity? Adaptability?
Friend Leopard wears his on his skin. Not so with me.
Mine's in my mind! Step up and I shall introduce
—Fresh from playing the Vatican!—
That glorious comedian
Me! I have rushed here, slick and spruce,
To this grand crowd, with jokes from capitals and court,
Dances, juggling, mysteries of every sort . . .
Come see me tightrope-walking, masked!
A hundred dollar value, only fifty cents—

Just reduced to five! A unique experience!
Money back if you don't agree, no questions asked!"
Monkey was right about diversity; when located
Only outwardly it quickly leaves us sated,
But it is the mind's most winning capacity,
Prodigal of brilliance that time cannot turn black.
Yet many a man parades with audacity
      With all his talent on his back.

5

The Schoolboy, the Teacher, and the Man Who Owned a Garden

(L'ÉCOLIER, LE PÉDANT, ET LE MAÎTRE D'UN JARDIN)

A stinking schoolboy stuffed with nastiness
Due to a stupid nature and like school
(For boys are stupid and boys' schools suppress
What they find of reason in each young fool)
Liked to climb fruit trees. This lord of misrule
Spoiled a neighbor's trees of fruit and flowers,
Thus depriving him of autumn hours
When his proud trees would hold Pomona's best,
Ripened and ripening, laden and blessed—
Thus spoiling spring when blossomed buds would lift
Before his eyes fair Flora's fairest gift.
One day he saw the schoolboy at his apish play;
He saw young shoots snap; he saw branches dip and sway;
Clumsy feet smashed buds that though delicate and slight
Promised to make fall rich by making springtime white.
The bark was scraped too, all with such fine disregard
      The outraged owner took it hard
And wrote the boy's teacher a letter to complain.
The teacher replied by coming, his class in tow,

Which made the garden seem to grow
Wild green boys in bunches. Yet his teacherly brain
        Never saw how this multiplied
        The boyish harm already done.
This was a punish lesson, he remarked aside;
They would see their error and learn in unison.
That was his lesson plan; it led him to long quotes,
Virgil piled on Cicero. The boys felt their oats
        As his sermon flowed on and on;
They kept busy, wrecking. Half the garden was gone
By the time he stopped and stopped the boys' exploring.
        I detest an eloquent don
    Talking out of place, endlessly boring.
        What's the world's worst beast? I know what.
    A schoolboy. Teachers earn the title too.
With even the better of the two, I will not
        Ever have anything to do.

6

The Sculptor and the Statue of Jupiter
(LE STATUAIRE ET LA STATUE DE JUPITER)

A sculptor bought a marble block.
"What will my chisel make of it?"
He thought. "A bathtub? A wine crock?
A god? A god? Lifelike, big, fit

To make the people shrink and stare—
A Zeus so real men will insist
Not stone but he himself stands there
With lightning staggered in his fist."

His work made good his word; when done
It seemed divine, beyond man's reach;

It was, or so said everyone,
A living Zeus in all but speech.

Even the sculptor was stricken,
They say, transfixed by such surprise
He thought the god might quicken
Right in front of his very eyes.

A like artless simplicity
Toward art makes poets create
Gods unknown to antiquity
Fearing violent wrath and hate.

Such arts are childish in this way:
Children suffer great vexation
If they think dolls with which they play
Are threatened with irritation.

As we think, so do we feel.
Thus the pagan's errors have spread
Made, by man's need of myth, half real,
Kept alive by his secret dread.

Deep are the joys men discover
In serving their chimeras.
Pygmalion becomes the lover
Of Venus whose father he was.

Man would gladly pay any price
To make real his inner desire.
Shown the truth, that man is like ice
Who at a lie turns into fire.

12

The Candle

(LE CIERGE)

On Mt. Hymettus*, zephyr-tended gardens thrived
In every cleft. There bees, being somewhat divine,
  First drank nectar sweeter than wine
And there, in the gone days of the gods, bees first hived.
When they had fled their castellated citadel
And rendered all its secrets amber up—or (why tax
  Our wits?) when the hive was just wax,
  The honey emptied from each cell—
It was melted. Beeswax candles would nightly flame
  Bright, lest the gods be left to grope.
One such candle saw how bricks when fired became
Durable and hard. Hard duration was its aim.
Like Empedocles** on that steep volcanic slope,
  Mad with hot dreams of lasting fame,
It dove for the fire. So much for baseless hope,
For which a lack of metaphysics is to blame.
All things differ in all ways. You must extirpate
The thought that others follow the same trail you're on.
The waxen Empedocles perished on the grate,
  Foolishly, o more than moron.

*La Fontaine notes: "Hymettus was a mountain praised by poets, located in Attica
[Greece], where the Greeks collected excellent honey."

**An ancient philosopher who, "through ridiculous vanity," La Fontaine notes,
to better understand the volcanic Mt. Aetna, threw himself into it, but "left his slippers
at the foot of the mountain" to assure his posthumous fame.

18

The Kite and the Nightingale
(LE MILAN ET LE ROSSIGNOL)

Kin to the falcon but useless to man, the kite
Is loathed by farmers for its predatory greed.
Once, boys saved their chicks from a kite about to feed;
It snatched a nightingale to soothe its appetite.
The bird begged for life. "Such an impractical crime!
My one gift is song; I'm a scant-fleshed, skimpy thing
      In terms of food. But I can sing.
Let me tell you of Tereus*, of love sublime!"
"Tereus? Who's he? Is he good food for a kite?"
"He was a king. His love slashed the air, so bright
It hurt sharper than hate, being animal and fierce.
Loose me, and hear his song; it will haunt your hopes, pierce
Pain with joy. Honestly. It always does." "Absurd,"
      The kite replied, shaking his head.
"What a way to talk to a predatory bird!
      Music's to food as stone to bread."
"But my song feeds kings!" "When a king catches you, you
      Sing; he may dine on what he hears.
      When a hungry kite catches you, you
      Die. Empty bellies have no ears."

*For King Tereus, see note to Fable III, 15, "Philomel and Procne" (p. 47).

BOOK X

2

The Turtle and the Two Ducks

(LA TORTUE ET LES DEUX CANARDS)

Once a witless turtle housewife found herself bored.
"I'm sick of this hole," she said. "I need travel so!"
Well, all hope for magic in going abroad,
And dream, if fenced in, of just how far they can go.
      Two ducks heard Wife Turtle; they soared,
      Discussed it, skimmed down and said, "Wife,
Behold, our limits are the sky. We can afford
      To elevate your house-bound life.
Let us lend you our wings and make your spirit free.
      You need culture, new sights to see,
New lands like far America, strange folk, strange speech,
Strange ways. Learn like Ulysses what wanderings can teach."
These were odd ducks. I've never before suspected
      Ducks and Homer were connected.
Wife Turtle beamed; she knew she was no drudge, not she.
The ducks quacked, "Grab the stick. When we take flight, we three.
      We'll free you from dull gravity."
They shouldered the stick and warned, "Those jaws mustn't budge;
They're essential as air to our ingenious scheme."
The stick between them, they bore the turtle wife high.
As they flew they heard an astonished people cry,
      "A flying turtle? It's a dream!"
      All three creatures felt wise and proud
As shouts rose from crowds below, "It's a turtle cloud!"

"A cloud turtle!" "No, hats off, men, for we have seen
        Royalty! There flies Turtle Queen!"
"Her? She's no queen!" came next. Wife Turtle yelled,
            "Don't laugh!
I am too a queen!" She'd have done better by half
To keep her snappy answers safely shut inside
For when she loosed her grip, spreading her jaws to speak,
She went to the ground with an earthly turtle shriek
And smashed; vanity had sabotaged her bold ride.
Vast vanity, no prudence, and speech far too free
        Plus idle curiosity
        Frequent each other; why shouldn't they?
        They're close relations, I'd say.

4

The Man Who Buried Things and His Friend
(L'ENFOUISSEUR ET SON COMPÈRE)

        A penny-pincher amassed more gold
        Than he dared house. Cupidity,
Sister and dear companion to stupidity,
        Made his mistrust every stronghold
        And strongholder; and yet, how he
Longed to deposit that wealth somewhere. This is why:
"Cash on hand tempts me to buy whatever I see.
        Spend means subtract, not multiply.
Therefore the likeliest thief of my gold is I."
Thief! why value gold above the joy it buys, friend?
Right use is not theft; gold is meant for men to spend.
        This truth I can certify:
Wealth is worthless till you enjoy what it can buy.
Take joy of life now; exchange your hoard for pleasure
While you may; after all, it costs nothing to die
But you pay as high to keep as to get treasure;

You buy with your life the bright dirt you deify.
Our miser might have sought a man
Whom he could trust, to be his wealth's custodian;
Instead, he buried it away from every eye.
A friend helped dig the hole deep in a hidden plot.
When, weeks later, he went to look, he found the spot
But nothing else; of gold, no sign.
"My helpful friend has helped himself to what is mine,"
He guessed; and ran to say, "Friend, I have one more pot
Full of gold. Help me hide it with the first, next week."
That night the first pot went back. "Who cares?" thought the sneak.
"Ten days from now I'll be twice blessed
When I dig up both pots. The old fool never guessed."
But the old fool had grown wiser.
He kept his wealth home, determined to employ it
Where he could at least enjoy it.
His false friend had no chance to become a miser.
Revenge of this kind is most sweet.
There is exquisite pleasure in cheating a cheat.

7

The Pheasant Hen and the Roosters
(LA PERDRIX ET LES COQS)

To a riot of roosters enclosed in a pen
Was added a mild pheasant hen.
Her sex, and the ordinary
Laws of decent hospitality,
Made her hope for that gallant cordiality
Roosters claim as a tribal speciality.
But the roosters proved more murderous than merry;
Careless of the honor of the aviary,
They showed the gentle foreign lady small respect.
Often enough she was painfully bruised and pecked.

At first her feelings were hurt, too,
Yet when she saw what the roistering boys could do
By way of civil war, claw to wing, beak to flank,
She consoled herself. "It is their custom," she thought.
"Let us pity, not scorn them. We have Jove to thank
                That natures differ, as they ought.
                Each species has its etiquette.
Roosters are roosters—a fact I need not regret
Since pheasants are pheasants. Would I were with them yet!
                However, we must not forget
Man, not roosters, keeps them and me penned. To catch me,
                To keep cocks, to house me here,
To clip my wings—these are man's rules. It would appear
That the one whose ways we may well despise is he."

8

The Dog that Had His Ears Trimmed
(LE CHIEN À QUI ON A COUPÉ LES OREILLES)

"Behold me whom these brutes misuse!
I guiltless am mutilated.
How long, master, will you abuse
Our patience? None dare oppose you." Thus orated
Bulldog Muffler. "You make a laughingstock of me.
                You turn my golden youth to dross!"
The kennelmen paid no heed to his bitter plea;
His ears got clipped while he still cried, "O tyranny!"
Disillusioned, he slunk away to mourn his loss.
Time passed. Muffler, who loved a fight, managed to see
The advantage of his ears' abbreviation.
He would have fled from many a battle station
                Bannered by the torn and bloody ears
That mark dogs of combative disposition.
The less dog left to the enemy's dentition,

The better it is for a bulldog buccaneer.
With a single target area to protect
      Attacks are easy to reject.
Muffler was so slick, his neck in a brass collar
His head with less ears than there's gold in a dollar,
      The very wolves showed him respect.

<u>12</u>

The Lioness and the Bear
(LA LIONNE ET L'OURSE)

      Hunters killed the cub of a lioness;
She howled and howled to proclaim her desolation.
      The deep woods shook with her distress
For which she, with great pride, refused consolation.
      Night that shelters all creation
      In shadow and silence, failed
To still her. Every living creature was impaled
Sleepless on the sharp grief shrilled across her nation.
      "Great Queen," an exhausted bear said,
      "We know you dine well night and day
      On those you honor as your prey.
      Have they parents, these honored dead?"
      "Of course!" "Yes? Then how can it be
That those parents refrain from howling in our ears?
      They keep private their bitter tears;
      Cannot you too mourn silently?"
      "Silent? I'm the bereaved, you know . . .
My son! Gone! Woe is me! He has left the world gray!
Fate killed me too, with his death-blow."
"The world is still bright. What makes you think in that way?"
"Fate! No fate was ever worse than mine!" Poor old fate—
Though each man who moans finds only his own heart wrung,
All men are prompt to blame fate with a common tongue.

Is there someone who thinks his grief uniquely great,
His sorrow such that it will never dim nor cease?
Let him remember Hecuba* and hold his peace.

*Hecuba, King Priam's wife. During the Trojan War, her husband and almost all
of her children were killed.

15

The Merchant, the Gentleman, the Shepherd, and the Prince

(LE MARCHAND, LE GENTILHOMME, LE PÂTRE, ET LE FILS DE ROI)

From a wrecked ship there crawled ashore
Somewhere in the New World they had hoped to explore
        A merchant, a gentleman, a shepherd, a prince.
        Newly poor, hungry, they soon learned
        What curt sympathy men evince
        Where others' troubles are concerned.
They had never met before they emigrated,
And their four pasts would fill books if fully stated,
        So let me start where they sit down
Around the public fountain of a little town;
They are half starved. They plan how to better their fate.
The prince holds forth on the anguish of those born great:
The shepherd counters, "The past is past. I suggest
        We forget it and do our best
To find work to do. Once we start, we'll get ahead.
        Together we'll soon earn our bread.
Griping is useless. Work is work, here or in Rome.
Let's get to work—first for food, then for passage home."
Might a shepherd talk like that? Yes! Does God read
Stud books when He gives out brains? Courts have their sages;
        Towns and farms have them too. Indeed,
Though sheep are a notoriously stupid breed,

Stupidity's not contagious.
Well: they heard him and at first, in their ways, agreed.
The merchant smirked. "These folk are uncouth, but well fed.
Let's found a school and get rich." "Rich. Rich!" the prince said.
"I'll teach civics. We're just what Americans need."
  The gentleman cried, "I shall spread
The most couth art of all, the art of heraldry!"
As if halfway to India the minds of men
Need the childish jargon of blazoned vanity!
The dismayed shepherd shook his head and tried again.
"Fine talk . . . but my stomach is deaf, men. Creation
Of a school would take months. I'm too hungry to wait.
  There is no fun in starvation.
  Your plan is good to contemplate
But where I come from 'First work then food' is the rule.
What shall we eat tomorrow? your plans for a school?
  This very day, who'll fill your plate?
We need food now. My plan is this: I'll go get it.
  Skip the talk; you won't regret it;
  The thoughts of hungry men lack weight . . .
Now if you'll excuse me, I'll see what can be done."
  The shepherd rose and soon had run
Into the woods. The kindling he gathered there bought
Two days' food for four. Fed, his friends no longer sought
In fantasies the satisfaction work can give.
Dreams may have charm, but to have them a man must live.
  My tale tells me this: never yet
Have dreams and schemes sufficed to keep a man alive.
  His hands, his back, his honest sweat
Are the natural tools by which man can survive.

BOOK XI

4

The Dream of a Man in the Land of the Great Mogul

(LE SONGE D'UN HABITANT DU MOGOL)

A man in Mogul dreamed he saw a Grand Vizier
In Paradise, enjoying a pure atmosphere
Of bliss infinite in its depth and duration.
The dream then showed at an opposite location
     A hermit hugged by flames so tight
The most wretched observer would pity his plight.
The dreamer found their lot oddly unexpected;
It seemed Minos* had confused the men and their fate.
He could not sleep, his astonishment was so great.
The dream was too strong and strange to be neglected;
     He sent to have it dissected.
The soothsayer said, "Your dream, unlike most, is not
Nonsense, nor is it hard to unravel its knot;
     The gods sent it to you as food
For thought, sire. In their hearts during their earthly years
The Viziers loved—and seldom obtained—solitude;
The hermit longed to please and frequent Grand Viziers."

If I might, I'd add to the soothsayer's good sooth,
And rouse men to love quiet retreats; for in truth
Such lovers possess, untroubled by self-conceit,
Pure, Heaven-born goods, springing new-grown at their feet.
Solitude, where I have known joy from my first youth
That I still cherish, shall I never come, and bar

The loud world from the shadowed freshness that you are?
Who would hinder me, alone among your dim aisles?
When shall I give my time, far from courts, towns, and styles,
To the Nine Sisters**, to instruct me in the skies
Whose divers movements are unknown to mortal eyes,
And in the names and strengths of those wandering gleams
That differentiate our lives, powers, and dreams!
At least let me—if such projects prove too immense—
Delight in stream-side flowers blooming sweet and dense;
Were my verses to paint them, it would be enough.
Fate chose no golden threads to weave through my life's stuff;
And the bed I've made is no rich, sumptuous puff:
Then do the joys of such a life deserve rebuff?
No. They are as deep, as prodigal of pleasure.
I vow Fate new tribute, pressed from desert leisure.
When the moment is come, and death and I have met,
I'll have lived without cares to die without regret.

*Minos, the legendary king of Crete, son of Europa and Zeus, served as one of the judges of the dead in Hell.

**The Muses, in mythology, daughers of Zeus and Mnemosyne (Memory) who presided over the liberal arts, including poetry, music, dance, philosophy, and astronomy.

5

The Lion, the Monkey, and the Two Donkeys
(LE LION, LE SINGE, ET LES DEUX ANES)

King Lion, wishing so to rule
As to need no apology,
Had Dean Monkey set up a school
For one, in graduate sociology.
In his opening lecture, Dean Monkey, M.A.,
Said, "Good government—that game great heroes play—

Demands the death of vanity.
Self-love is the curse of our common animal day.
What eats the public good away?
Clannish, race-proud inanity.
A ruler free of vain intent
Will triumph in just government . . .
But self-love is subtle; chased, it will reappear
Masked as the virtue you revere.
Its standard line of last defense
Parades the pigs and wolves of greed as plain horse sense.
Fame crowns your reign, o wisest King,
Because you scorn thin-skinned false pride
That takes offense at every silly thing."
"Thanks, Dean. Now—protocol aside—
Speak," said the king. "Say what you mean."
"Sire, every race and profession
Including my own," cried the dean,
"Has a self-praise device: to claim group possession
Of wisdom, feigning modest surprise
That we too, as members, are wise.
We sneer at difference. We call others' gifts crude.
Our group produces greatness—that's our theorem.
We heap praise on our own kind. Since self-praise is rude,
We praise ourselves in praising them.
Therefore, sire, from these premises we may conclude:
Tricks and poses make some reputations stately;
Such shifts to seem superior, special, occult,
Though they may fool fools, do not fool the wise adult.
I walked near two donkeys lately.
They were swinging incense, like all the group-proud cult;
Clouds of praise poured from each to the other in turn.
I heard one ask, "Sir Donkey, dos not your soul burn
At the wrongs of that beast the texts call highest, man?
Unjust and dull himself, he takes our name in vain
To mean—pardon, I must speak plain!—

A stubborn dolt, a fool, a clown, a charlatan.
          Worse! Man, that deaf barbarian,
Calls "blaring brays" our eloquent laugh, speech, and song,
Yet congratulates himself on his own squeaked noise.
Could they but hear your voice, sir, they would blush like boys
          Caught out, overwhelmed, bad, and wrong.
They would squeak no more—but enough of dwarf-eared beasts!
          You speak; I hear; my spirit feasts . . .
          You sing; I forget Philomel;
Your musical inventions weave a magic spell;
You're better than Stravinsky combined with Callas;
Frankly, you're diviner.' Said the other solemn ass,
'Milord, these are the points where you yourself excel—
A true donkey!' Well, they walked far and wide that day
          (Though they'd gone far enough, I'd say!)
Praising their tribe, each other, and thus themselves too.
So do fools fan each other's pride. I've known a few,
Not donkeys either, but persons of power and fame;
          Not content to be called by name,
They would skip from ducal 'Lords' and 'Excellencies'
To the exchange of 'Majesties' if they but dared.
I have gone too far, perhaps, sire; but if you please,
          These are my true thoughts. They are bared,
Your Highness, in the hope they may serve you somewhat;
Your royal mind can make my poor thoughts fit for use.
This lecture has dealt with group pride and its abuse
          By fools whose 'I have; you have not'
Aims at others' pain, but makes them ridiculous.
Self-love causes injustice too. I may discuss
Injustice next, and how justice may be restored."
He may have, at that. Or perhaps the Dean non vult*,
Being respectfully unready to insult
That most awesome of kings, his leonine lord.

*Non vult. (Latin) to not want.

8

The Old Man and the Three Young Men

(LE VIEILLARD ET LES TROIS JEUNES HOMMES)

An old man had orchards planted.
Three young neighbors warned, "Your time is short; you're eighty.
For you, a work of such scope is far too weighty.
    How can you take for granted
    You'll live to see these saplings grow?
You're a senior citizen, a patriarch;
Have dignified retirement fun. Sit in the park.
Don't work so hard. Relax, let go.
    Why slave just to benefit your inheritors?
Dismiss your ambitious longings. Turn to the past,
Hope is a burden age may abandon at last.
The future's no concern of yours."
    "Nor yours!" came the old man's retort.
    "Real value, no matter what a man's vocation,
Develops late and slowly, and its stay is short.
Young and old, we're all in the same situation:
Fate's pale hands hold each and every thread.
Which of us will stand in sun, when the rest lie dead?
You say at night, 'Day will come.' True. Time continues—
Will you? Death won't fear your youth, your plans, your sinews.
Someday my great-nephews may eat fruit from these trees.
    It is my right, if I please,
To give pleasure to men whom I may never meet.
The thought of them is my reward, and it is sweet;
It flavors this day and many to come, maybe.
    Who knows how many dawns I'll see
    Decorating your tombs with day?"
He was right. One of the young men left on his way
To America, and drowned within sight of port.
One joined the army to earn power, gold, and praise;

He and his men were ambushed and his life cut short.
The third, grafting a tree, fell and ended his days.
      The octogenarian wept
      To think they would never grow old.
He had cut in marble, above them where they slept,
      The story that I have just told.

EPILOGUE

In this way, alongside these clear waters, my Muse
     Translated with heavenly tongue
     All things said or whispered or sung
In the voice of nature that countless creatures use:
     Go-between for them all and each,
I have dressed them as actors to play in my verse;
     For every creature has its own speech,
     None are dumb in our universe.
Their eloquence surpasses what my verse can reach;
If those I mention find me not faithful enough
If, as a model ideal, my work is too rough,
     I have at least opened a door
Which others may employ, opening it still more.
They, blessed by the Nine and to the task committed,
Will demonstrate lessons that I have omitted,
Cleverer lessons, still hidden fabulously.
You, I know, are busied far more marvelously.
While my harmless Muse has toyed with calm enjoyment
Louis took Europe; he now makes his employment
The noblest proposals a king has ever shown.
     Blessed by the Nine beyond mere rhyme,
He, his triumph, his projects, in themselves alone,
     Utterly vanquish Fate and Time.

"The Old Cat and the Young Mouse" (Book XII, 5)

Fifth Part

BOOK XII

5

The Old Cat and the Young Mouse
(LE VIEUX CHAT ET LA JEUNE SOURIS)

Miss Mouse, young both in years and experience,
Addressed old Champ Cat with tears and soft eloquence
Hoping to move him to mercy, though she was caught.
     "Let me live, do. I'm small. I'm short.
     I survive at no one's expense.
     Surely your household can afford
     The grain a day that is my board.
     A whole walnut once made me sick!
     Truly. It made me look, my lord,
     Like a pumpkin tied to a stick.
Time will augment my stature. Commute my sentence,
And I'll make a tasty feast for your descendants."
The old cat cleared his throat and addressed his captive.
     "Cats my age are not adaptive.
You young ones think talk can change the fate of nations.
A deafening gulf roars between generations.
An old cat, merciful? I've never heard of it.
     Die, and tell the Fates your sad tale.
    As for me, I must say I fail
    To understand a word of it.
As for my sons, they can fill their own dinner pail."

He ate the mouse. To my mind
This shows both silly, self-satisfied youth basking
In the thought that the world is theirs for the asking,
    And hateful age, hard and unkind.

6

The Sick Stag
(LE CERF MALADE)

Deep in deer country an old stag fell very sick;
    The word got round and friends flocked thick.
Most of them kindly and firmly offered to stay
To comfort him. He said, knowing their motives base,
    "If you don't mind, I'll die my way.
    Enjoy your tears some other place,
Please. Let me welcome death with sober decency."
    But with insistent clemency
They cheered his calm to bits, and said while doing so,
    "One more for the road—then we'll go."
    To stags this meant they'd eat some more
In the near glens. Grazing night, day, and in between
They stripped their dying friend's neighborhood of its green;
They left, then. The wretched stag had been ill before
    But had his grass to nibble at.
    Still sick, now he was worse than that,
    Sick and a pauper. At the last
    Starvation ended his hard fast.
    Those who offer comfort are prone
    To make the comfort all their own.
    Dutiful love has dropped from view;
    Selfless kindness has vanished, too.

II

The Eagle and the Magpie

(L'AIGLE ET LA PIE)

An eagle, queen of the upper air, soared gently
Near lower-class Meg Magpie, who watched intently,
           Immensely
     Afraid of the eagle gentry.
Though Meg's opposite in rank, mind, and temperament
The well-fed eagle gave her kind encouragement:
"Fear not! Jove himself, when bored, beneficently
Condescends to lesser creatures; consequently
     I who serve him condescend too.
Just be yourself, Meg. Amuse me. Tell me what's new."
Mere Meg, all aflutter, came obediently
With her trivial chatter of who can guess what.
Horace sang of one who said unspeakable things;
Meg Magpie said them all, plus some that he'd forgot.
Hopeful, despite the stage fright royal presence brings,
She then proposed her busybody flitterings,
     Her ferret's mind, her rapid wings,
To the queen's secret service, as spy. "I think not;
     Your world cannot reach into mine,"
     Indignantly shrilled the eagle.
"Let us remember, though I choose to be benign,
     I am, and you are not, regal.
     Your gossip nothing can refine.
     Farewell." Relieved, Meg watched her go.
Life with the godlike great may be harder than we know.
Plain mortals, called to enter it, will find inside
No dearth of spies and gossips who grin and grimace
To hide the spiteful falsehoods they spread every place.
Men at court must either wear their turncoats with grace
     Or, like the magpie, be born pied.

13

The Fox, the Flies, and the Hedgehog

(LE RENARD, LES MOUCHES, ET LE HÉRISSON)

Through the woods there wandered an old inhabitant,
      Fox, the clever, the elegant.
Stricken by hunters, he had survived, but endured
A plague of flies. He had no rest from their attack
      That hovered on his bloody track.
Dodging, he mourned the fate that thus caricatured
His own vanished quickness, now grimly mirrored back
      By the alert and darting pack.
"See how they cling to me, who has often outrun
      And always out-thought all the rest.
Am I a cow? Is a fox the food flies like the best?
They defy even my plumed tail. What's to be done?
May the gods swat you! Begone, uninvited guests!
      Rude unmitigatable pests!"
      A good hedgehog, hearing him curse
      (Note: hedgehogs are new to my verse)
Thought she might deliver him or at least give pause
      To the buzzing distress flies cause.
"I'll spear them by the hundreds with my darts," said she.
"You'll do better without them, Neighbor Fox. Trust me."
"No," said Fox, "though I thank you. Do no such thing, please.
Let them be. Let them finish their meal at their ease.
They are already half full. If this lot goes,
More will come. Nothing is worse than fresh, hungry foes."
I fear our own world does not lack such parasites;
Rich and poor, weak and strong, provide greed's acolytes.
Aristotle himself applied this tale to men.
      Fitting instances are widespread
      Here and now, perhaps more than then.
Bakers are not safe with those who have little bread.

14

Love and Folly
(L'AMOUR ET LA FOLIE)

Love's a mysterious science.
Consider the Cupid myth. That cherubic youth
    Wins hearts, not the mind's alliance;
    Logic rejects that kind of truth.
But just now I am not logically minded;
What I want is to give my version of the day
    Aphrodite's son was blinded.
What cut off Cupid's light, though gods guarded his way?
(Note: I don't say the deprivation did no good.
It's not my place to judge, though I think lovers should.)

He—still keen-eyed—played with Folly one vacation;
They scored their games with fierce Olympic precision
And so fought. Cupid said, "I want arbitration;
    I'll accept the gods' decision."
    Folly cried, "No! Fight me or quit!"
Then, when she lashed him in wild derision,
    Luckless Cupid lost his vision.
    Aphrodite witnessed it.
Did she shriek her maternal grief? You know she did.
    Gods held their ears; from Nereid
    To Zeus, deafened Olympus hid
But found her pleas for vengeance too shrill to ignore.
How she mourned Cupid, who must tap his sightless way
Because some people's children can't behave at play!
She insisted Folly must suffer forevermore,
Though even so, no fair atonement could be made.
    The court sat; the facts were displayed;
Public interest was weighed, and that of the invalid.
The gods pondered and passed sentence, with legal pride:
    Thenceforth, forever, so they bid,
    Folly must serve as Cupid's guide.

18

The Fox and the Turkeys

(LE RENARD ET LES POULETS D'INDE)

Fleeing from a young fox's teeth
A clutch of turkeys made a tree their citadel.
Sir Fox besieged them from beneath,
 Sneering at their scared sentinel.
"Fool! do you suppose that your imported nation
Now makes its perch beyond the law of creation
That says foxes shall eat fowl? You'll learn!" Learn they did.
The moon was full; young Sir Fox wished it were hid;
New at sieges, he thought darkness advantageous.
But hunger honed his wit and made him courageous.
Spotlighted by the moon, he performed for the fowl;
He faked climbing, falling, collapsing with a howl;
He died on the grass, then jumped up resurrected.
 The foxy clown he confected
 Was as supple as Harlequin.
He spun; he danced, until as he expected
 He saw his audience begin
To show signs of being bizarrely affected:
They perched atilt, hypnotized by constant gazing
 At one thing, and it amazing.
More and more bemused, the turkeys began to drop.
The fox danced and killed until, working without stop,
He had stocked his larder with half the flock to eat.
Our own fear delivers us up to what we dread.
To focus on danger makes us weak-spirited,
 Helpless, and easy to defeat.

20
The Scythian Philosopher
(LE PHILOSOPHE SCYTHE)

A born extremist, both Scythian and Stoic,
Sought to observe life somewhere else, less heroic.
He went to Greece and met a venerable man
Like Virgil's Tarentian sage*—tranquil, satisfied,
The equal of kings, the gods' mortal suffragan**;
Like the gods, healthily self-possessed and clear-eyed.
A quiet garden and its care gave him pleasure.
The Stoic found him there, pruning with due measure.
He lopped off dead wood and cut back shoots to provide
His fruit trees with a balance by which they surpassed
      Their natural disposition,
For to trim excess growth increases fruition.
The Scythian demanded, aghast,
What prompted the sage to this wanton destruction,
For, "Time sickles life soon enough. Why interfere?
Since death harshly regulates nature's production,
      Wisdom bids man must hold life dear."
The sage said, "I do not kill; I prune. Reduction
Of the rate of growth makes flourish what I do not shear.
      'Nothing in excess' rules me here."
The Stoic, back in his somber Scythian home,
Pruned too, and thinned flowerbeds down to the bare loam.
He then proceeded to teach his friends and neighbors
      To imitate his Greek labors.
Fruit trees were pruned short with heedless incompetence;
Grape vines still in growth were sheared too short and too soon,
      Heedless of time and moon
      Heedless of logic and good sense.
What was left died. So Stoic sternness may transgress
      Stoic precepts against excess
      And indiscreetly may destroy

All desire, all passion, good or bad, in the soul.
        With these parts gone, what is the whole?
I do not like those who fear man's longing for joy,
For if the motive force of right desire be shed
A man may survive but he might as well be dead.

*Tarentian sage. An industrious old man in Virgil's "Georgics"
(book 4, lines 125–146) who makes infertile land fruitful through his labors.

**Suffragan. A subordinate bishop assisting a diocesan bishop in the Anglican church.

22

The Madman and the Wise Man
(UN FOU ET UN SAGE)

A madman chased a wise man, hurling stones. "Well thrown!"
Cried the wise man, stopping. "Here is my last coin, friend.
You deserve far more for the efforts you expend.
To lovers of justice, like me, it is well known
That working men, like you, deserve a living wage.
See that rich man? Stone him! He's no impoverished sage."
The madman obeyed, liking remuneration.
The rich man, however, took his lapidation
        As a sharp and brutal insult;
He did pay for it, but his terms were difficult.
His servants quickly closed out the madman's account,
        Beating him for twice the amount.

Men just as mad may haunt the courts of kings;
They make the ruler laugh at your expense.
Never force them to halt their sly babblings
Unless your own power is immense.
Instead, gently persuade them to attack
Someone ready and able to strike back.

TALES AND SHORT STORIES

"Another Story Taken from Athéneus (The Glutton)"
(Part I, 8)

PART I

5

The Story of Something that Happened at Château-Thierry (The Shoemaker)

(CONTE D'UNE CHOSE ARRIVÉE À
CHÂTEAU-THIERRY [LE SAVETIER])

There was a shoemaker whom we'll call Blaise
Who wed a beautiful girl as wise as he.
Since they were short of cash and out of maize,
They asked to borrow grain for a small fee
From a rich dealer with a one-track mind.
He looked them both up and down, and agreed:
But when repayment was due, he grew less kind.
Lord knows why. I know too: he went, indeed,
And asked payment plus interest from the bride.
"All things considered, top, bottom, and side,"
He leered, "you've got what it takes; I'll forget
Your loan, if you'll just put me in your debt."
She smiled. "I'll think it over, if I may."
When Blaise heard the dealer's proposition,
He liked the part that meant he needn't pay.

"Good!" he cried, "He thinks he's paid admission
To a fair! Wife, what hurts worse than owing?
Paying back! He'll see what my fair's showing.
Tell that hog the performance opens here;
Invite him, and say he won't find me here.

Start the show—and ask for the IOU
Well before the last act. He'll take your cue.
When the note's yours, warn me. Cough good and strong.
Cough twice, in fact; it's worth it. I'll rush in.
We'll both be all right, and he'll be all wrong.
We'll owe him nothing, and prevent a sin."

It worked. Blaise brought the dealer local fame;
The whole town laughed at the sound of his name.
One market day, a rich butcher sniggered
In public, "Madame Blaise, I'll be jiggered,
You cheated yourself with that cough, you know.
Why didn't you signal after the show?
Then instead of going off half-triggered
You'd all have gained. Blaise would never have known."
"O sir," she sighed, "we're poor, and dense as stone."
She bowed to his wife, who was there with friends.
"Your ladies' wits begin where my wit ends.
Their advantages and mine can't compare.
I know your own wife, here, isn't like me;
She does what you describe, sir. But be fair!
All of us can't be as clever as she."

6

A Story Taken from Atheneus
(Venus Callipygus)

(CONTE TIRÉ D'ATHÉNÉE [LA VÉNUS CALLIPYGE*])

Two sisters of ancient Greece both laid claim
To the finest, fairest rear of their time.
Which tail forged ahead? which bottom's true fame
Topped? Which back was in front, which terce most prime?
A judge chose the elder girl's back matter;
Her finish was more fine and far fatter.

She got the prize, and his heart; soon they wed.
"But the younger's sitter's not a smatter
Less meet; I'll marry her," his brother said.
It went so well, their joys were so perfected,
That after them a temple was erected
In honor of Venus Callipygus.
No other church—though I don't know its rite—
Could so, from head to epididymis,
Move me with deep devotion to its site.

*Venus Callipygus. Literally, "Venus of the Beautiful Buttocks," after nude statues
of the Roman goddess Venus—whose name itself means "charm" or "beauty"—
found in palaces in ancient Rome as well as at Versailles, in La Fontaine's own time.

8

Another Story Taken from Atheneus
(The Glutton)

(AUTRE CONTE TIRÉ D'ATHÉNÉE [LE GLOUTON])

A glutton wanted to dine
On a sturgeon, whole and entire,
Stuffed, then roasted in good wine,
Served headless, hot from the fire.
He ate it all; but he burst.
Doctors, failing, said, "You should
Make ready; expect the worst;
Now's your last chance to make good."
The glutton gasped, "I'm resigned;
But friends, while still of sound mind,
I do have one last request;
Hurry, now, and grant my wish:
Serve that head! Before I rest
I'll finish my splendid fish!"

PART II

I

The Ear-Maker and the Mold-Mender

(LE FAISEUR D'OREILLES ET LE RACCOMMODEUR DE MOULES)

William bid his pregnant young wife remain
Safe at home when business called him away.
His wife Alix was a girl from Champagne,
Naive, pretty, and inclined to obey.
Neighbor Andrew sometimes walked out her way
(Why, God knows, and so I need not mention).
A trapper, gifted with sly invention,
Andrew spread few nets without success;
To fly full-feathered from his wit and skill
A bird would have needed more cleverness
Than bird ever had or bird ever will.
Guileful, shrewd, or wily, Alix was not;
Nor used to games of love-me, love-me-not,
Where the two who pursue are both pursued.
Her way was, "Forward," without detour;
She had no experience, aptitude,
Or appetite for worldly-wise amour.
So with William gone about his affairs
And Alix at home alone upstairs,
Andrew came to call. He spoke up boldly,
Eying her clinically and coldly:
"Why! How could Will leave you in such a case
And rush away to such a distant place
Without finishing the child you expect—
Which unmistakably still lacks an ear!

From your color I easily detect
The classic symptoms; the case is quite clear."
"Oh, no!" she cried. "Heaven forbid my child
Should be half deaf and also oddly styled!
What now? Have you no remedy, no cure?"
"In your case, I do have . . . though to be sure,
Help is not something I often supply;
Most people's troubles never trouble me—
My neighbors excepted; for them I'd die;
No effort is too great, as you will see.
But why waste words? It's high time to proceed
With the remedy for that ear you need.
Just let me put my talents to your task."
"Make sure they match," she said. "That's all I ask."
"My neighbor's welfare is my own," said he.
"The ears will match. You have my guarantee."
She, her density tactful, nice, and fit,
Was pleased to find him set up to cure her
When he showed his skill, to reassure her.
If she lacked brains, they never noticed it.
So Andrew toiled away with tender care
Gently kneading the second of the pair,
Attentive to each soft-skinned shadowed fold
Of flesh and cartilage set her and there.
"Good!" he said. "Tomorrow we'll try the mold
Under varied stresses of use and wear;
Then we'll smooth it to its binaural best."
She said, "I'm grateful for your interest.
It's fine to have neighbors to rely on."
He rose next day with workmanlike zest
Ready to test and carefully try on
What guileless Alix thought of as an ear.
"I've left my work," he told her, "to come here
And carry on." She said, "I'm glad you could;
I almost sent to ask you to hurry:
Until that ear is in place, I worry."

As they worked she did whatever he would
Or wouldn't; they both did a great deal,
So much, that sweet Alix began to feel
Her cares might not be cured but multiplied.
"The child does need more than one ear," she sighed,
"But what if it turns out to have twenty?"
"No fear. Daily treatments will do the trick.
After I make this ear, and make it stick,
There'll be two ears exactly—that's plenty."
The treatments were kept up faithfully till
Alix' husband came home, his business done.
When he had kissed her, she scolded, "Oh Will!
How could you leave me with a child begun
And not finished? You must thank our neighbor!
He dropped everything else and worked long hours
On a second ear for this child of ours
Which you left incomplete. You must go, Will,
And thank our friend in need; for you know, Will,
A better friend than that is hard to find."

Dumbfounded, William could hardly believe
Anyone, even Alix, was so blind.
He made her repeat her recitative
To determine at what he must laugh or grieve—
Till, burning with rage and dismay combined,
He snatched up his sword with a mighty heave
And threatened to kill Alix on the spot.
Wide-eyed, she truly swore she felt no guilt
And begged that innocent blood not be spilt.
He sheathed his sword; she wept, "O tell me what,
What have I done wrong? I haven't been rash;
The ear cost you nothing whatsoever;
You'll find the full count of your goods and cash . . .
And as for your locus beneath my sash,
Andrew explained that he isn't slap-dash;
You will be better received than ever.

See for yourself, Will. There's nothing to hide.
I have not harmed you! Kill me if I've lied."
William, simmering down, said, "I'll admit
There was nothing wrong with your intention.
We needn't waste our breath discussing it;
What you suffered was misapprehension.
Listen: I have one more thing to mention:
You must send for our friend tomorrow, wife,
And fix it for me to catch him upstairs.
Now, since I mean to take him unawares
Do not warn him—if you value your life.
Be cute! Make Andrew think that my business affairs
Have called me off for a second session.
Let your message give him the impression
You have something to ask of him alone.
And when he comes, chat in a friendly tone—
But not about that ear. You have my word
The ear is completed, more than completely."

Simple Alix obeyed most discreetly—
Which does not surprise me; I've often heard
Fear makes even donkeys shrewd. Andrew came,
Went upstairs; and Will followed, soon and loud.
Andrew sought a way out, three being a crowd;
There was none. He dove between the bedframe
And the wall and . . . waited, abruptly tame.
Will knocked; Alix opened the door in fright
Wordlessly pointing to where their guest hid.
Will had come so armed, he could have bid
Four Andrews surrender without a fight;
Instead, he left in silence with Alix.
Outside, he breathed, "With men to hold him tight,
I needn't kill him; it's vengeance I seek
I'll lop his ears . . . better! I shall wreak
True revenge, by lopping as do the Turks,
A tribe famed for fittingly cruel works."

Having shocked his poor wife, Will locked the door
Which was the room's sole exit, from outside.

Andrew grinned; though still trapped and forced to hide,
He wrongly supposed he need fear no more
Since Will seemed to be without suspicion.
Will smiled too, at what he was planning for;
"Do as you're done by," was his ambition;
He would avoid degrading public noise
And crush Andrew with more than counterpoise.
"Alix, go tell his wife your tale," he said.
"She'll understand what I was raging for.
Tell her to come at once or evermore
Be guilty of the blood I threaten to shed.
Say that I have in mind a punishment
Drastically hard on her environment;
Explain that ear-makers of Andrew's sort
Are paid off, according to my report,
By a deed that makes your hair stand on end
To imagine. Tell her that I insist
She be the sole witness of what I intend;
Suggest that though I refuse to desist
I might agree to change the punishment
To something easier for them to bear.
If you succeed, you can be confident
I'll forgive and forget the whole affair."
Alix did her best. In came Andrew's wife,
Running hard for the first time in her life;
She thought Andrew must be locked up somewhere
When she found no one but Will in the house,
Upstairs, where there was no sign of her spouse.

Will watched her rush up, breathless and alarmed.
He invited her to sit, and disarmed,
Before he explained, "I always maintain
Ingratitude's a most pernicious vice.

Andrew worked for me, and gave me advice.
Before you leave, I'll make my thanks quite plain
By returning the favors he bestowed.
He made Alix an ear, so you are owed
Something similar. It occurs to me
Your children all suffer a small defect—
Their noses are too short; it's plain to see
Their mold has a fault, which I shall correct;
I can re-line molds with great expertise.
I therefore suggest that we if you please
Inlay that mold." He got up from his chair
And set the mold's container with some care
On the bed behind which Andrew still stayed.
Topsy-turvy, Will worked the part he played;

His patient subject as he corrected
Rejoiced, for his fury was deflected
From her spouse to herself; no wife could be
More full of wifely charity than she.
As for Will, it was plain to hear and see
He was too righteously aroused to be
Willing to skimp. Andrew's wife was repaid
More than whatever Andrew had laid out—
For grapes, melons; for drops, a cascade.
"Revenge is sweet," was proven beyond doubt.
Since it was honor Will wished to restore,
He chose both to give more good than he'd got,
And to donate it by closing a door
Much like the one that had opened the plot.
Mutely Andrew endured, trapped on the spot,
As the mold was poured, inlaid, and embossed.
He was lucky that this was all it cost.
Some subtractions reduce the brave to fear;
So though Andrew gained what everyone scorns,
He gladly exchanged that imagined ear
For the addition of a pair of horns.

6

The Vindicated Servant Girl
(LA SERVANTE JUSTIFIÉE)

Boccaccio's not my sole supplier,
Though he most often satisfies my needs;
Sometimes I grind the grain I may require
At other mills, from other growers' seeds.
Well used, wheat from any field makes good bread;
This time not Italy but France instead
Supplies me, from an ancient, royal source.
They're the old but novel novels, of course—
Great tales, great writing, worked out with great skill
By the Queen of Navarre. A hundred times
She wrote, "C'était moi,"* and wove her naive rhymes
Into those rare tales that charm us still.
Now, forget who wrote the plot first, or how.
As always, there are bits added by me.
If changes were outlawed and I less free,
I'd quit my tale-telling job here and now.

Under her master a maid learned love's game
On her time off from housework for his dame.
She was a beauty, a bed-bedighting prize,
Apt at learning where the seat of learning lies.
She was good goods, as the French more or less say.
The lady of the house slept late one day
While her husband strolled in the garden shade.
He was not surprised to meet his wife's maid
Who had gathered flowers in a bright bouquet
For her mistress whose birthday was that day.
He said his touch would make it sure to please;
He'd add the "wealth of globèd peonies"
Just then in bloom blush-white and rosy-tipped
In her blouse. His hand somehow slipped inside;
She leaped in self-defense. The blouse tore wide;

Two fair blossoms bounced where the cloth had ripped.
Such games advance by delay and defense;
To see and not to touch is to make intense
The wish to touch. Next she pelted him blind
With roses in constant fire, soft and dense.
He lunged for her, without ambivalence,
But even kisses would not make her mind.
To teach her a lesson, he pressed for more;
Learning, she fainted on the flowered ground;
He took care of her three and brought her round.
But their luck turned. A spry gossip next door
Watched their game, plays and innings, and kept score.
Our hero somehow spied the spectator.
"Caught," he groaned. "Unforeseen, unforefended,
That viper-tongued trouble-loving beldame
Has seen us practicing our friendly game.
I'll fix her! No breech but may be mended!"

He left to demonstrate what he intended.
His wife like himself had just then risen.
"Birthday bride, come out of this dark prison!
You and I shall gather flowers," he said,
And led her out to the same flower bed.
Surprised though not shocked, she gave him his head.
The game resumed. He had much the same luck
With his novel partner. Few plays were new;
He sought fresh blooms till all the flowers flew;
Dancing breasts sprang free, with floral tips to pluck;
And once again the grass got trammelled flat.

Later his wife paid calls, in her best hat.
Her neighbor welcomed her with special glee
Disguised as pitying severity.
"My dear, dear friend; my poor, poor dear;
If what I have to say is hard to hear
It's for your own good. It's about your maid:
Kick her out, and soon. How you've been betrayed!

After all you've done for her, too, the slut!
She thinks herself a lady, by her acts.
Dump her back where she came from. That vile hut
Is just her style. Be brave, dear. Facts are facts.
After what I saw today there's no doubt
You owe it to yourself to kick her out.
This window, where I just happened to be
This morning, overlooks your garden, dear . . .
I was sunning myself. What did I see
But your husband—and who should appear
But that hussy, tossing flowers! First she . . ."
The wife smiled with relief and cut her short.
"Oh, that's it! I know. The hussy was me."

NEIGHBOR

But listen! for once they were really caught.
I truly hesitate to tell you this—
Well, for each flower she plucked he plucked a kiss
And when she'd done she'd picked a rose tree bare!

WIFE

I tell you I know; that was me, down there.

NEIGHBOR

They went from flowers and kisses, share and share,
To bodice buttons; my word! such a pair!
He soon had his hands full, you understand?

WIFE

Since I'm his wife . . . there's nothing he can't do.
Why, can't your husband do as much with you?

NEIGHBOR

Then she fell and somehow managed to land
On a cushiony bed of grass . . . Well! Well!
What's this? You're laughing?

WIFE

It was I who fell.

NEIGHBOR

White empty underclothings flew, and then . . .

WIFE

What could I do?

NEIGHBOR

Can you honestly swear
That you, not your maid, kicked that underwear?
Do be sure, for if their play had been prayer
I'd say they kept at it right through "Amen."

WIFE

Sure? Why yes. I know what I do, and when.

NEIGHBOR

Oh, I'm glad; accept my apology.
I've been too proud, perhaps, of my good eyes.
I'd have sworn to her physiology
As displayed both with and without disguise.
But forget it. You'll keep her, I suppose?

WIFE

Why not? She gives us excellent service.

NEIGHBOR

As you say. Ah well, that's the way it goes.
Isn't it nice that you aren't nervous.

*In the fifteenth story of L'Heptaméron by Marguerite de Navarre (1492–1549), a prose collection inspired by Boccaccio, the phrase "that was me" (c'était moi) is also repeated by a character for comic effect.

II

The Villager Looking for a Calf
(LE VILLAGEOIS QUI CHERCHE SON VEAU)

An anxious young rube walked round in a wood
Looking for a calf that had gone astray.
He climbed a tall tree as high as he could,
And peered and stared for clues to the calf's way.
A lady and her love came, kissed, and stood
Beneath that tree, by a convenient stream;
While making her easy on the soft green,
Loud at the sight of what he saw, cried he,
"O joy! what joys I see! What don't I see!"
But didn't specify what *what* might be,
Within his joyous vision on the mound.
He sat up fast, though, hearing from the tree,
"Please, sir who sees, do you see my calf around?"

PART III

8
The Load
(LE BÂT)

A jealous artist always used to paint
An ass on his wife's navel when called out.
To find it untouched later soothed his doubt.
His colleague, who loved the wife, found that quaint,
And once when he had somehow erased it
Took up a brush and neatly replaced it.
He was sure his memory could not fail,
But his ass did differ in one detail:
It was loaded; the first had gone bareback.

The husband asked to look, when he got back.
"You should trust me, dear. The ass proves my case.
See?" she murmured. When he saw what she showed,
He cried, "Blast the two of them, blind and base—
Your ass and him who left it with that load!"

9
A Kiss Returned
(LE BAISER RENDU)

Jack left church with his new wife at his side;
A gentleman saw, liked, and stopped the two.
Said he, "Where did you get this lovely bride?

Let me kiss her; I'd do the same for you."
"Gladly," said Jack without further ado;
"Sir, she's at your service here and now."
The kiss Jane got brought blushes to her brow.
A week later the gentleman was wed;
Remembering what he had forfeited
He let Jack kiss his bride as he had said.
Jack gasped with joy. "Seeing how just you are,
Sir, I regret but one particular—
When you kissed Jane as we agreed you could
I can't help wishing, once you'd gone so far
You'd gone right on while the going was good."

10

Epigram
(ÉPIGRAMME)

Alice was ill. An officious friend said,
"Confession is good medicine, I've read.
Shall I send for a priest? They're so calming."
"Good! get dear, good Father John—so charming—
A saint!" cried Alice. "For spiritual things
I always turn to him. His soul has wings!"
A boy ran off to the rectory door
And said, "Please, it's Father John I've come for.
Alice wants him to hear her confession.
He's her regular confessor, you see."
The lay brother bowed with grave discretion.
"It's Father John Alice wants, son? Dear me,
Her spiritual adviser's Father John?
But he's in a better parish than we—
He died and was buried this ten years gone."

PART IV

8

From "King Candule"
(LE ROI CANDAULE)

A man is his own best tool for wrecking his life.
        King Candule found this hard to learn.
He was stupidity itself; he could discern
        The loveliness of his young wife,
But urged his servant Gudge to see her and confirm
That beauty. "Gudge, look upon her. You must agree,
So far you've seen just her smooth face and soft hair;
The best of her is hidden. Why take it from me?
Shapes. Colors. Firm. Well, you haven't seen a thing, see,
        Until you've seen how she stands there
                Small, stripped bare.
I can prove it to you, too, without her knowing.
        You'll find out why she's worth showing!
Only . . . don't get ideas. No touch-and-going,
        Know what I mean? No instant itch,
        No nonsense, you know, not a twitch.
        She's my wife, Gudge, mine, understand?
        No love games, backhand, underhand.
I know you're an artist, a critic, Gudge my man,
        So I trust you; all artists can
Look at naked girls as if all that flesh were clay.
        Just as an artist, you can say
If any statue ever made or thought or planned
Has a more stunning body to the expert eye
        Than this of hers that I have manned.
I left her in her bath. Come on, so you'll know why
        I'm the luckiest king around."

They went. Gudge looked, if "looked" can mean the bright-hurt daze
    Of ecstatic sight that Gudge found.
    Lusts laced his blood in arrowed rays.
He could not seem indifferent, for all his skill.
    He would have liked to keep quite still,
Hide his feelings and contemplate that effulgence,
But lest the king translate such silence as ill-will,
He spoke. He chose a critic's terms of reference,
    Or a salesman's, broad and intense,
A knowing catalog of vague hyperbole,
Not cold, not hot, not too personal. "I state
Jove himself made do with less than you. What legs! Great!
What hips! Great! What silk! What connubiality!"
    From where they hid the queen, of course,
    Could not hear his bold discourse;
    It would have shocked and shamed her ears.
    Women were uncultured then.
    Those were underdeveloped years;
    Now they're civilized as men,
    Such crude praise though it be broad
    Thrills the female citizen
    Who finds no compliment untoward.
Gudge the king's man looked world-wise; Gudge the inner man
Gazed on glory and grew weak, strong, Vesuvian.
The king, vaguely doubtful, led him away—too late;
    Each trait had its sweet duplicate
    In his desire; each dip and swell
    Woke longings distance could not quell.
    Love pangs can only be made well
    By love, that cure, that malady.

Before the king, Gudge affected propriety
But the queen guessed his passion, caught clue after clue,
    Till she knew;
Worse, she knew its source. Her peculiar lord the king,
    Laughing, told her everything.

Did not that idiot know
That women should never know
Men laugh at them bawdily?
Though pleased by rough jests she must
Pretend she is orderly,
And feels disdain and disgust.
This queen did rant, gaudily—
For her wrath was real and true.
Her fury only dwindled
As hope of revenge kindled
Fantasies of what to do.
Readers, become, I beg of you,
For the moment gently sexed:
For the turns the queen's thoughts took
Would leave male minds too perplexed.
She thought: "What eyes dared see
My most secret secrecy?
Common eyes should not by rights
Feast like gods on divine sights—
(Or like my king: right, divine,
And here! head of a real state!)
Paradise to a potentate,
Common men are none of mine.

Revenge!" thought the queen. "Revenge!" Sparks began to fly.
She fed the sparks shame, wrath, dismay; she watched them burn.
She heaped love on the flames too, I understand. Why?

Why, all emotions serve one turn.
And Gudge, that handsome lad, was easily excused;
It was by his tempter the queen had been abused . . .

He was a husband—a great crime
That makes men guilty, win or lose,
No matter what discretion they use,
And the punishment is capital, every time.
See where feminine logic has led us, my friends.
The queen now loves Gudge. Her husband king is despised,

Though he will be immortalized

On Don Juan's list which never ends;
His is an honor seldom sought but oft bestowed.
Having matriculated in stupidity,
Candule was graduated as Bachelor of Naught—
Fair enough. However, the queen's avidity
Made him take—in physics—a graduate degree.
To help him, what big brandy bottles the queen bought!
    Death was what she wanted him taught;
    Death's diploma would set her free.
    She held a quart for him to drain
    In one great gulp; it burst his brain.
        One king fell; another rose.
        Gudge won the queen. The king's clothes
        Fit him both for bed and throne;
        He ruled upright; he ruled prone;
        He was happy. But suppose
        He had stopped to think, and seen
        Who now husbanded the queen? . . .

II

Smoked Eel
(PÂTÉ D'ANGUILLE)

Even beauty, best though it be,
Will stale at last like daily bread.
Tired of white? Try rye instead.
My device is, "Diversity!"

That butter-crust girl pleases me—
Why? because she's new. This one
White as a milk-loaf split when done,
But too long in my company,
No longer shakes my apathy.
She strikes me pianissimo;
Her heart says yes; my heart says no;

Liking lacks all logic, and so,
My device is, "Diversify!"

I said it first some time ago,
But differently, to testify
I practice this best rule I know:
My advice is, "Diversify!"

Another man who kept this rule
Married a glorious beauty;
In time his ardor grew so cool
More-than-love turned less-than-duty;
Wedded plenty of possession
Simply smothered his obsession.
His valet had a wife as well,
A rather sweet one, honey-lipped;
The master, who was well equipped,
Soon played the clapper to her bell
Until the valet chanced to see
Changes rung like a symphony
And called his tuneful wife away.
He called her more than that, that day,
Waxing foolishly eloquent,
Treating the trivial event
Like some bizarre unheard-of curse.
God grant we suffer nothing worse!
He made his master hear his moan:
"Sir, Moses and Reason both are wise
In teaching us: to each his own.
Your wife—unlike mine—is a prize
Who'd make even a statue rise
To salute her, for all its stone.
With the joys you monopolize
Why search for other exercise?
You honor my wife to excess;
She deserves humbler happiness.
Yours is yours; mine is mine. What need

To draw from others' wells? That's greed
When yours brims full of what's required.
Think of the thirsts she has inspired!
Had God granted me such blessing
As is yours for the possessing
In your wife, I'd be so serene
I wouldn't diddle with a queen!
Done is done; and what must be, must—
But I do hope you will amass
Domestic vintage so robust
(I speak without offense, I trust!)
You'll drink no more out of my glass."

The master said nothing, wryly.
He called his cook and commanded
The man be thrice daily handed
The dish he rated most highly;
No lesser dish might he be served
Than fine smoked eel, as he deserved.
The grateful valet cleaned his plate
The first two times. By the third meal
His palate was in a sorry state,
Sick at the very smell of eel.
He ached for something else to eat.
The cook replied to his appeal,
"Our orders say you get this treat
And nothing else, at every meal.
It's a great honor. Have some more!"
"Eel, eel! what do you take me for?
I'm hungry. If serve eel you must
Then don't trouble to have it smoked.
Roast it. No? . . . Friend Cook, I'm half choked;
Let me have plain bread. No? . . . A crust?
Some old crumbs? . . . What am I to do?
Bread, by God!—by the Devil, too!
Devil take this damned eel as well!

If eels be safely shut in hell
I'll get to Paradise, somehow!"

His master came up, and exclaimed,
"How can our favorite food be blamed
For your fickle appetite now?
Your dish of smoked eel is a prize
That makes every appetite rise;
What would Moses and Reason say
Of appetites that so soon change
From coveting to frank dismay?
Recently I made an exchange
For which you blamed me. I suggest
You think about my lack of zest
For a morsel most men esteem.
Your present surfeit is, I deem,
Like mine. Now, how strange does it seem?
My friend, remember this advice:
To satisfy your appetite
Vary your bread, rye, dark, and white.
Diversity is my device!"

The valet was consoled to hear
His master make the matter clear;
He might have made it clearer, though—
For as a man of parts he knew
More than that which mere infants know,
"I like change." So? What else is true?
This is: If you are set on changing,
The hope of gain may gain the hearts
Of owners of replacement parts;
Spare no effort in arranging
Exchange of goods, rather than theft.
This advice is so effective
And that master's methods so deft
I'm sure he added collective

Cure-alls, that healed his valet's breach
By adding to his golden speech
The weight which wins accomplices.
A golden tongue accomplishes
More for love than anything. Yet
I must repeat lest you forget
A warning that never grows old:
Change should always be made with gold.
Golden words, and not words alone,
Will gleam to win her chaperone,
Her dog, her best friend, her. Some find
The gleam makes even husbands blind.
Our valet did not at first seem
A likely victim of the gleam
Yet he lowered his last defense
For modern golden eloquence.
Beside it, even Chrysostom*
And old Demosthenes** seem dumb.

Jealous no more, the valet learned
To be glad that his worm had turned.
He eagerly, from that time since,
Took whomever he could convince
For a change. He judged all creatures
By the newness of their features;
He chose those new to him, at least;
The newer they were the better.
Each day he dreamed of some new feast;
Each day he fared forth to get her:
Maiden or mother, wild or kind,
The tigers, the quick deer, the mice
Bid him sup where he had not dined.
Diversity was his device.

*St. John Chrysostom (c.347–407 AD), a preacher given the name
"golden-mouthed" (Chrysostom) because of his eloquence.
**Demosthenes (384–322 BC), an Athenian politician and orator.

OCCASIONAL VERSE

"The Fox and the Grapes" (Book III, 11)

LETTER TO RACINE, 6 JUNE 1686

June 6, 1686

When Poignan returned from Paris, he told me my silence had distressed you—especially since you had been assured that I have been constantly at work since I came here to Château-Thierry and have had a head full of verse instead of a mind addressed to my business affairs. Of all that about half is true: my affairs occupy me insofar as they deserve, that is, not at all; yet the resultant leisure is filled not by poetry but by laziness. I received just after I came here a letter and a verse stanza from a little girl only eight years old; I have answered that and it is the most energetic act of my stay to date. . . .

The letter and verses together—if what I hear from Paris is true—took the young lady not more than half an hour's time. She now and then puts something about love in her verses without knowing what love is. Since I saw I should get no peace until I had written something for her, I sent her the following three stanzas, set to the same tune as hers.

> Paula, your verses and letter
>   Prettily written to me
> Are good but might well be better
>   Were there signs of love to see.
> The Muse learns love as love appears
>   In the heart's experience.
> Patience, Paula, in three more years
>   You will see the difference.
>
> You use the word but do not show,
>   Paula, love's reality.

I hope one day to see you know
    More of Cupid's mastery.
Of sweet sighed converse you ignore
    Both the sweetness and the sense . . .
Paula, when spring has come thrice more,
    There will be a difference.

If naive grace be here, if we
    Praise the child's sweet little voice,
What may we hope when, lessoned, she
    Can make a more lively choice?
In such verse, your wits demand
    Heart to give them eloquence.
Let three springs, three snows, cloak the land,
    And you'll see the difference.

So you may judge, Sir, if there's any cause to be displeased that I do not send you the wonderful stuff that I write. I had also promised a letter to the Prince of Conti; it is at present in the works; the following lines will be part of it:

Learning makes a fool a bigger fool—whom I flee.
    Wherever one is, I won't be.
    I'd sooner see the sharp swords drawn
    By men to mortal anger born
    Than watch a dolt pick up a tome.
    Ronsard is harsh; he lacks nice choice,
Lacks taste, orders words badly, spoils with his French voice
The infinite graces of ancient Greece and Rome.
Our good elders let him get away with it—
They couldn't get enough of eruditious wit
Which we now think a vice; today no man dares speak
In classical references more than once a week.
When Chance does bestow them, you must use them neatly,
Choose among them, and learn their contexts completely,
While knowing that for all your pains they may not please.

You'll hear, "His work needs footnotes and parentheses!
He may be well-read, but writes as if ill at ease.
Let him conceal his learning; then his wit may shine . . .
Racan was a primitive, yet his work's divine!"
That is how they talk, and not without relevance,
Malherbe could use classic allusion more than we
For in his day the Court did not yet openly
      Offer homage to ignorance.

    I trust you will recognize that since I am sending you these lit-
tle scraps, any notion that I am being secretive with you is false.
May I ask you, however, to refrain from showing them to anyone,
for Madame de la Sablière has not yet seen them.

ON THE DEATH OF MOLIÈRE

(SUR MOLIÈRE)

Plautus and Terence lie under this stone
Though only Molière was placed in the grave.
One wit fused three talents; that one wit gave
France joy in great art, noble and her own.
They are dead! I shall not, I fear, be shown
Their like again; though some have skill and worth
None will long compare with these we have known.
Terence, Plautus, Molière are gone to earth.

EPITAPH FOR A LAZY MAN

(ÉPITAPHE D'UN PARESSEUX)

As Jean came, empty-handed, so he went,
Both income and capital used and spent;
He considered gold too trifling to keep.
With his time, however, he took more care,
Dividing it in two parts, fair and square:
One for doing nothing, and one for sleep.

ANOTHER EPITAPH
ON A TALKATIVE MAN
(AUTRE ÉPITAPHE, D'UN GRAND PARLEUR)

Here lies Paul in his last bed
Who babbled of wonders for years.
Praise be to God, rest to the dead,
And peace on earth to our poor ears!

INDEX OF FABLES AND TALES

TALES AND SHORT STORIES

ABOUT THE TRANSLATOR

Marie Ponsot, whose collection, *The Birdcatcher* (Knopf, 1998) won the National Book Critic's Circle Award, is also author of *True Minds* (1957), *Admit Impediment* (1981) and *The Green Dark* (1988). She is a native New Yorker who has enjoyed teaching in graduate programs at Queens College, Beijing United University, the Poetry Center of the YMHA, and Columbia University. Among her other awards are a creative writing grant from the National Endowment for the Arts, the Delmore Schwartz Memorial Prize, and the Shaughnessy Medal of the Modern Language Association. Her *Springing: New and Selected Poems* will appear from Knopf in 2002.

ABOUT THE EDITOR

Benjamin Ivry is author of a poetry collection, *Paradise for the Portuguese Queen* (Orchises), as well as biographies of Rimbaud (Absolute Press), Poulenc (Phaidon), and Ravel (Welcome Rain). He co-translated Adam Zagajewski's *Canvas* (Farrar Straus & Giroux/ Faber & Faber) and translated *Albert Camus: A Life* (Knopf) and *Memoirs of Balthus* (Ecco).